Pleasure Extraordinaire 4

Liv Bennett

Pleasure Extraordinaire 4

I love a man who doesn't want me, and the man I detest most is ready to give up his promiscuous life to be with me.

The final pieces of the puzzle are coming together to reveal one of the most shocking secrets from the past. The bricks of the unbreakable wall of Hawkins Media Group are falling one by one.

Who will die? Who will survive? It all depends on who is willing to risk everything.

LIV BENNETT

CH 1 - The Used-up

"Just like that, baby," Zane purrs in my ear. "Take all of me inside you. Fuck yourself on me."

His eyes are hooded, but following me intently. Damp brown hair clings to his forehead. I can't help noticing how handsome he actually looks with his two-day beard and moustache curling around his full lips. His skin looks darker somehow, perhaps because of the dim light in the luxurious Summer Suite. Even the lights inside the Pleasure Extraordinaire villa are modified so the escorts look irresistibly sexy.

Zane's hands find my waist as he bucks his hips up, pushing his cock deeper inside me. I take in a sharp breath, trying to relax my muscles to take his full length into me.

Ace is standing only a few feet behind us, his presence pushing my senses on high alert. I'm torn between listening to what he is about to say and fighting to ignore the awakening desire in my sex as Zane's cock inches deeper and deeper toward my core.

It's wrong--heart-wrenchingly wicked! Ace watching me while I'm riding Zane is a sin big enough for me to burn in the deepest pits of hell, but there's no level to describe the depravity of me enjoying Zane's cock. I purse my lips to swallow the sounds of pleasure seeking to escape my mouth.

Unsuccessfully.

My head falls on Zane's shoulder as we hump each other with an animalistic desire.

"Lindsay!" Finally the reaction I've been expecting from Ace comes. His voice is deafening and layered with pain. "What the fuck are you doing?"

I'm sorry. Please understand me. I want to yell and go down on my knees to ask him for forgiveness and explain it's all for his wellbeing and that I'm being forced into it.

Zane is staring at me with a nasty expression, as if reminding me to keep my part of the deal. Only he can stop Michael and Edward. Only he can save Chloe, Ace, and me. He has a plan. More important than that, he knows Michael's ulterior motives for hiring me as his pretend girlfriend, and through him I'll have a chance to protect Taylor if she's the one targeted in Michael's plans.

I should do it. I should let Zane take his stupid revenge from Ace. Even though Ace must be going through shock and disgust, it's nothing in comparison to what Edward can do to him.

My stomach twists and I lose my focus at the thought of Edward cornering Ace when he was a kid. Did he show up in his room in the middle of the night? Waking him up from a sound sleep to push him into a trauma? Forcing him to grow up too soon and get a taste of life's horrible facets too early? If it were possible to shelter the little Ace from that horror, I wouldn't think twice before signing a contract with the devil himself.

I hear Laila's soft voice. "Let's go, boss."

"No," Ace yells. "Lindsay!"

Zane tightens his hold around my waist and digs his fingers into my skin, his eyes focused on my face. I get what he's trying to say.

"Go, Ace," I say rather harshly. "There's nothing here for you to see."

Zane conveys his praise with a smirk and cups his hand around my neck, pulling me down for a kiss full of biting and licking. The sounds coming from our lips are disgusting to say the least, but I let Zane enjoy the minutes with me while he can. His hands are running through my hair, his lips fully claiming my mouth. His cock is rubbing all the wrong places inside my sex, making me squirm with more lust.

I will Ace to go and stop exposing himself to more ugliness, because what will come next won't be pretty. I'm moaning and riding Zane faster and it's not even acting. Zane's cock is doing an excellent job of making me lose my logic, and I hate him for doing this to Ace.

Footsteps follow curses and the door closes with a loud bang. At last Ace is gone and his soul won't be crushed with witnessing me being fucked to orgasm by another man. Not just any other man, but his goddamned brother.

"You did a good job, baby. I'll reward you with a mind-blowing orgasm," Zane whispers to my lips.

No, please, anything but that.

He delivers exactly what he promises. He wraps his arms firmly around my waist and pounds his cock into me. Over and over again. For minutes long, without having to take a break or slow down. Ace must be cursing the sexual training Zane has undergone at Pleasure Extraordinaire.

Tears well up in my eyes for what's coming. Just last week, I promised Ace I wouldn't fuck another man, but here I am, slowly progressing toward a mind-blowing orgasm. My eyes close as I gradually come to terms with the fact, but then, all of a sudden, Zane slides out of me and tosses me onto the bed. Before I can grasp what he's doing, he flips me around to get me face down and grips my hips, displaying my ass up in the air.

"Fucking bitch," he growls as he thrusts back into me forcefully. "Admit it, you love my cock. Say it, you whore."

I remain silent. I might have gotten into a degrading deal with him, but there's no way I'll admit what he wants from me. For that, I get a stinging smack on my buttocks.

"You don't want to talk? You think it makes you less of a whore, huh? No, sweetheart. You're no different than the professional hookers who do it for money. You may think you love Ace, but your vagina is soaked with my cock."

Another blow on my buttocks, and I have no choice but to scream in pain.

"Shut up," I yelp with both pain and anger and pull myself down against the bed to free myself from his hold. How dare he speak to me like that, when I'm only doing this to protect the people I care about?

Zane loses his balance and collapses over me on the bed. Taking advantage of his distraction, I elbow his ribcage with all the power I have. "You're forcing me into this, you jerk, and you're calling me a whore? If I'm a whore, you're a pig full of shit. You're no different than your father. Both delusional men blinded by power and money, who think you're better than anyone else, but you aren't worth a damn shit."

His body doubles over in pain from my blow, and I push him and roll to the other side of the bed.

"Oh, no, you're not going anywhere." He quickly regains his posture and catches me by my arms, pulling me against him. "Your cunt hasn't had its fill of my cock, yet."

"Let go of me. You're hurting me." I fight back, but his hands are glued around my wrists, and the distorted look on his face tells me he's getting extra pleasure out of my helplessness.

"Open up that little pussy for me or I'll have to open it up myself and it won't be gentle." He moves over me, pushing all his body weight against me. His cock is hard and slick between our sweaty bodies.

I struggle to breathe under his weight but continue to wrestle against him. Despite all my efforts, though, he is way too strong for me and manages to hold both my hands above my head. Although I try to push him away, his other hand finds its way to my legs and pushes my thighs apart. His torso is heavy on me, preventing me from moving. I can barely breathe.

"You like it rough; I'll give you rough."

I feel his hand sneaking between my legs and his fingers teasing my entrance. Shame fills me as I feel more juice soaking my slit at the touch of his fingers, and I turn my head to the side to at least escape his stare.

He pushes two fingers, maybe three, into me without any warning. I bite my lips to stifle the scream. I see he's enjoying being forceful with me, and I won't give him the pleasure of seeing me coming apart.

His fingers are sliding in and out of me rhythmically. Every time they're out, he glides them over my clit down to my backside, and then back inside me again. I have to shudder at the multiplicity of the explosive points he's setting off on my flesh. I don't see any inkling of slowing down from Zane's side, and if he doesn't stop anytime soon, I'll climax in multiple locations, something that has never happened to me.

"Yeah, baby, enjoy it while you can. Ace won't want to do anything with your used-up cunt, anymore." Zane breathes against the moist skin of my face, distracting me from the upcoming orgasms. Is he doing it on purpose?

Working me up close to a climax, but taking it away from me in the last second? Ignoring his bullshit comments, I turn away and focus on the sensations going wild in my sex. The sooner I get off, the faster it'll be over. At least that's what I hope.

I bite my lower lip as the ecstasy starts rolling across my body, and close my eyes and witness the flowers blossom in the darkness, while a furious wave of orgasm hits various points inside my sex reaching out to my clit.

This could have been a beautiful, divine moment if it wasn't forced on me in such an ugly way. I'd have thrown myself on my lover and showered him with thank-you kisses for minutes on end for letting me experience these delicious explosions. I'd have cried and even declared my love, if it was given to me by Ace.

I don't do any of them and just keep the wild emotions bottled up inside me, hoping Zane won't see how successfully he can handle my body. But, he must have noticed my orgasm, perhaps through the convulsions inside me, because he's now on his knees and hovering over me, getting in his position back between my legs, his fingers still inside me.

"Look at me when I fuck you."

My eyes snap open and I'm confronted by Zane's face only an inch away from mine. My crazy mind is likely making it up but, rather than angry or hostile, his expression is of worry and regret.

He slowly pulls his fingers out of me, smearing my juices across the lips of my sex up to my mound, as if trying to show me how much he affects me.

"I didn't mean any of those words," he whispers apologetically, his warm breath tickling my skin. He rests his weight on his elbows on either side of my body so I'm not crushed beneath his weight. "I'm sorry if I hurt you. I was only trying to distract you from Ace and make you focus on me." His eyes flicker from my eyes to my lips and back. "This isn't a game, Lindsay. I'm not trying to hurt you or humiliate you. I'm not doing this to take revenge on Ace. I just want you to see Ace isn't your only option and that I can make you experience something special too."

I'm shocked to say the least, more so for the soft gaze of his eyes that are full of pleas and hurt. If his intention to have sex with me was really based on his feelings for me, then he has absolutely the weirdest possible way to realize his plan. Then again, why am I even surprised at the ways he chooses? He recorded a sex tape of me with him to save me from the contract with Michael. If that's not one of the weirdest ways to help a person, then I don't know what is.

"I can't stop thinking about you since the day we met. Since the moment you punched me in the elevator to be exact." A wry smile appears on his lips, and I can't help but grin, too, as I remember how I nearly came to injure him that day. "I know it'll sound uber cliché, but you're different from all the other women in my life."

The other women. God knows how many of them there are. I start to turn away, but he gently grips my chin to hold my gaze.

"You're the only woman who could see past my last name and money. You've always made it hard for me. I've never begged a woman for sex, other than you. You make me work for it, and I kind of like doing my best to please you. You're the only woman who doesn't make me think that I'm missing out on all the other fish in the sea. You're in my mind 24/7, and it makes me happy. It literally makes me want to jump up in the air and smash my feet together." He chuckles, caressing my chin with the tip of his thumb.

I swallow hard, trying to absorb his confession. I can feel his words aren't a way for him to fool me, but are honest and come from deep down in his heart. He might be a good actor, but not that good. Even if he's being completely honest with me though, what he's saying isn't some earth-shattering information.

"I'm so desirable in your eyes because I'm with Ace and you can't have me. A typical male behavior," I point out, hoping he'll see through his own character, but he shakes his head, dismissing my explanation.

"That's not true. I had no idea you were with him until I saw you two in the restaurant. I was on fire for you much before then."

"Is that so?"

He nods.

"Then, you were just sharing the fire with Tiffany Jordan that night, I assume."

He chuckles again, leans down, digging his head where my shoulder meets my neck, and takes a deep breath. I feel his moist lips and shudder inside as he places a soft kiss on the side of my neck. "I was only trying to prove to myself that what I felt for you was something temporary, and could be weaned off with sex—lots of sex."

"If you were a lawyer in court right now, you'd be losing your case. I don't want to picture you having lots of sex. That was actually the main argument I had against you. I'm not one to share."

"What do you say? Would I have a chance with you if I didn't have my other lady friends?" He lifts his head and faces me again, but this time the close proximity is oddly welcoming.

"Yeah. I guess so. But it doesn't matter anymore. I'm with Ace now." I say the last words as sweetly as possible, but obviously my method is without success, because the playfulness of his expression is replaced with one of despair and agony in an instant.

"You don't know Ace well enough to be sure he'll have only you in his life. Has he promised you exclusivity?" Zane asks. I open my mouth to answer him, but close it quickly, because to be exact, Ace hasn't told me anything about his plans to swear off other women for me.

Taking advantage of my silence, Zane speaks my mind. "He didn't and likely he won't, because he can't. He's running a business in the sex industry. He'll be constantly surrounded by women of every type. That doesn't speak well about him. Whatever you have with him is still very young, and restraining him from having other women will backlash. But not with me. If you pick me, I promise you here and now, I won't sleep around, I'll dedicate myself to you. I'll be the kind of man you deserve; honest, loyal, and respectful. Will you give me the chance to prove myself to you and to start over again?"

Ace and I might not have been openly exclusive, but that doesn't mean he'll go around fucking other women. His only disadvantage is that he's not here to defend himself against Zane's smear campaign. And, none of it matters anyway, because now I see, my heart beats only for Ace. I don't know what's wrong with my body for getting off around another man's fingers, but I'm Ace's and nothing can change that.

Zane is staring at me expectantly, but I can't, for the love of God, tell him what he wants to hear. "I...I can't do that."

The soft expression freezes on his face for a moment, and I wonder whether he actually heard my answer. Then, his features twist with hostility.

"I'm sorry, Zane," I add in a hurry. "It's too late."

"It's never too late."

Nothing is worse than a man who won't take no for an answer.

"Give me a chance and let's destroy Michael together."

Oh, the Michael threat again. How nice of him to remind me of it so subtly. Are we back on our deal from earlier--him helping me out in exchange for a sexy night with me? If only I could ask him directly whether he'll help me out if I openly tell him he doesn't stand a chance with me as long as Ace is alive.

"I'll go ahead and start the process tomorrow. It all depends on a yes from you."

Now it's not just a sexy night that he demands, but my affirmation to have a relationship with him. "What do you want from me exactly? Relationships don't start off with blackmail. However subtle yours might be, it is blackmail nonetheless."

"Then, let me show you how great it can be with us if you give me a chance. Allow me to make love to you the way I feel for you, but you have to promise me you won't think of him meanwhile. You'll be completely mine with your body and mind. Can you do that for me?"

Like I have an option to say no. "Okay, but first I want to know why Michael hired me. What does he want from me?"

He shakes his head as expected. "I'll tell you afterwards."

After what? He's clearly pushing me into a corner to make love to him. Where is love if it's forced upon you? Defeated and tired of this game, I nod my acceptance, and that very second, he lowers his head and kisses the corner of my lips.

"I fucked you hard." He lingers slowly on my lips. "I

fingered you." He places another kiss on the other corner of my mouth. "I licked your sweet pussy, but I never made love to you. In fact I've never made love to any woman. You'll be my very first." He raises his head to glance at me with scorching lust darkening his eyes. "Are you ready for it?"

Breath catches in my throat at his words. I hate how well he knows how to get me where he wants me to be. I whisper, "Yes."

With that, he moves back down to my lips and sucks them until I open up for him. His tongue is warm and invasive but doesn't urge me to puke this time. After a few minutes of inner-struggle, I give in and wrap my hands around his neck to pull him closer to me and start sucking his tongue vigorously. This is only Zane and me. The way I envisioned having him since the first time I saw him.

Only now I notice his cock has been flaccid all this time, but as our kiss deepens and becomes more passionate, his cock regains its fullness and length and pokes against my mound.

I lift my legs and lock them around his waist so his cock falls right between the lips of my sex. He rubs it alongside my moist flesh, intensifying my pleasure tenfold. My breathing gets louder together with my moans every time the head of his cock hits my entrance.

His hands skim over my breasts, cupping them hard. How shameful is it of me to want another man's cock? I couldn't have stooped lower. But the other part of me can't help thinking what would have happened to Zane and me, if he had embraced his interest in me from early on and ditched the other women in his life.

Would Ace still have any appeal to me? It's a challenging question to answer, particularly because

Zane's cock is now clearly asking for permission to enter.

He stops, pulling back. "I want you so badly, Lindsay. I'm dying here for your attention. It's killing me that you're still thinking of him." His eyes close with pain.

How can he know that? "I'll stop now. I promise." I'm not sure if I can hold onto that promise, though. Every second with Zane is proof that I truly belong to Ace, and it's sad that Zane doesn't want to see it.

"Then open up your pussy for me."

I nod quickly, nervous about the imminent seconds. His hand sneaks between our slick bodies and grabs his cock and then all I feel is his massive size shoved into me.

My mouth goes dry with the power of his thrusts, and I squeal at the stinging sensation between my legs. He promised this would be making love, but it's hard fucking all over again, because he's pounding into me, forcing me toward yet another raw and quick orgasm.

I have no idea why my body is so willing while my heart bleeds as the peak of the rapture approaches. I attempt to reach down for my clit to quicken the process, but Zane stops me halfway and takes over the rubbing. His thumb rounding my clit does the trick and I feel explosions setting off one after another inside me.

I let myself moan with pleasure and grab onto his shoulder tightly, but there's no way to hold back my tears from falling. I'd be devastated if I saw Ace having sex with another woman; how sad must he be right now, knowing Zane will use every trick under his belt to get to me?

Zane's thrusts become frantic soon after my climax wears off. Beads of sweat coat his forehead. His cheeks flash a bright red. His glazed eyes are locked on mine, conveying the promises of a sex-filled, loving reunion if I let him.

Wrapping his hands around my shoulders, he plunges into me with hard and loud strokes and then finds his release, shooting his thick load into me. A new wave of defeat settles deep in the pit of my stomach as I feel his warm fluid spilling out of me, marking me, dirtying me.

Ace won't want me again. Zane was right. He won't want anything to do with my used-up sex.

CH 2 - The Illusion - ZANE

Pain.

That's the dominant sensation I feel every time I'm around Lindsay. The first day we met, she shoved her elbow into my ribcage accidentally, as she was stepping in the elevator and I jumped in right behind her without her noticing me. I remember my eyes moistening from the pain of her slim arm nearly ripping through my bones and trying not to show it to her.

Next time I saw her, which was at a restaurant for lunch, a different type of pain rippled up inside me. When she explained to me her dismay against number seven, I seriously noticed my heart pinching with compassion for the hurdles she must have endured in life. Just like I did.

I knew her on paper, from her birth weight to the schools she attended, as a part of my job, but hearing the events directly from her lovely mouth, observing the world through her bright eyes, made it all so real.

She was like a rose growing among weeds, resilient and robust no matter what the weather conditions were. She was me, only in a seductive female body. And that realization made the pain in my heart grow together with the need to protect her and provide her with help. The help I never received from others.

I could cope with those pains, but not the kind of pain that clenched my guts when I saw her with Ace. Among all the millions of men in L.A., it had to be my fucking bastard brother who claimed a stake on her.

I could forgive him for having to share my mother's love with him, but not this. He was aware of my weakness for her, yet didn't refrain from seducing her.

I admit I wasn't entirely guiltless. Like Michael once said, 'When you notice a treasure, jump on it before everyone else notices it.' He meant it for stocks and bonds, but it was very well suited to Lindsay, too.

I was a complete idiot for not pursuing her before Ace could get his claws into her. I foolishly thought I didn't need another distraction in my life and indulged in sex with a variety of women.

In fact, in the days following having lunch with Lindsay, I screwed a record number of women to get her out of my system. The more pussies I tasted, the less pleasure my body seemed to be capable of registering.

It took a relatively long time for me to realize Lindsay had me totally under her spell. Actually up until the day I had her pussy for me to devour, I thought I could cure myself of her. That explosive day in the Pleasure Extraordinaire suite, then in her apartment, the realization struck hard; my heart was infected with the terminal Lindsay disease.

'How did I notice it at all?' you'll ask. Easy. Normally I never want to screw a girl for the second time. When I do it, it's only because the cock is hard and needs some warm and moist folds to dip into, regardless of their owner.

But not with Lindsay.

The first time with her was explosive and addictive, like the first blow of high-quality marijuana blunt. You inhale it once and that's it for you. Get ready for a life of cravings.

This is a game, and like every game, if you're focused and smart enough, you can turn the tables around and get the winning hand.

In this case, Edward's perversion assisted me in getting the upper hand. Not that I'd let a maniac like him molest anyone, be it a random waitress of a roadside joint or the man who stole the girl I want. But, that fact won't keep me from using my power to win Lindsay's heart.

She has set an unbreakable barrier around her heart, perhaps to shield herself from more pain. Also, she's nauseatingly stubborn. I'd admire that trait of hers if it was me she was keeping in her heart, but it's Ace, and because of that, I have to use every dirty trick to break the unbreakable and sneak into her heart.

I couldn't care less if it was Ace or the president of the United States watching us having sex. Making Ace jealous didn't quite make it to the top of my agenda. My real purpose to demand that condition from Lindsay was something totally different.

Brick by brick, I had to make her believe Ace isn't her only option. It was not Ace, but Lindsay herself, whom I wanted to show that I can arouse her. And arouse her I did.

Her body is the definition of responsive, calling out to me. And it's hot as hell, particularly because she's fighting against it with all her will ... and losing the battle. If only her mind was as easy to manipulate as her body.

Getting her from the point of wanting to puke at our kiss to the point of having her pussy convulse around my fingers was a success worth celebrating forty nights and days. And that with Ace still in the picture ... not to mention the short amount of time it all took.

The only way to deal with a stubborn person is mirroring her behavior. Just continue playing your cards until all her guards fall. That's what I'm doing right now. No matter how much pain her expression is hosting, I'll continue demanding a chance.

If she doesn't give in with the first attempt, she'll eventually fall for it as the game progresses. Patience is one of the virtues I was forced to develop by living the hell of Michael, and for Lindsay, I have an unlimited supply.

Laila. A bi-sexual, red-headed hottie. Always willing and never really faking it. I heard about her fame a long time ago and always wanted to have a night with her, but never really got a chance thanks to Ace's house rules.

When Lindsay called her for help, I thought 'I cracked the jackpot.' Two of my all-time-favorites will fuck each other then let me fuck them. I must have some kind of fairy dust sprinkled on me. However, time was ticking and I had to hurry for the grand finale of the short-lived love story of Ace and Lindsay.

I had Laila ride me first, quite aware of the sparks brightening Lindsay's eyes at the sight of our fuck. However, entering Laila's body had only proven one thing to me. That it was still Lindsay I wanted to have. My cock hardened more for Lindsay's tongue on my balls than Laila's squeezing folds around my shaft.

This is batshit insane. Me, desiring a girl I already fucked while having first-time sex with a beauty who could easily be a Victoria's Secret model? Something is sickeningly wrong there. No one warned me about the crucial fact that certain women can cause random sex to lose its appeal. Lindsay is the only woman who has managed to reduce my sexual desire for other women to zero.

But, as astonishing as it might be, as long as she insists on Ace, I'm doomed to the darkness.

I wish it was me who makes her eyes beam with the light of love…whom she stubbornly keeps locked in her heart…whom she puts her own dignity on the line for.

Lindsay's stubbornness isn't all bad, actually. Now that she's convinced of my role in rescuing her chicken-shit boyfriend, she'll get coaxed into anything I demand.

Without hesitation I can name the moment Lindsay kicked Ace out of the suite with mere words, as one of the handful of triumphant moments of my life. Her accompanying moans just moved it to the top three. The first two spots are reserved for the moments I'll ruin Michael and his twisted-minded boyfriend.

The harder Lindsay fights to close her heart against me, the harder I strike back, although it hurts to see her struggle to accept my affection. The other women in my life—in my past, to be absolutely correct—would readily lose a limb to have me begging them for a chance in their hearts, just like I'm doing with Lindsay. A grand irony or perhaps life's plan to get back at me for all the hearts I've broken with my selfishness.

My mind goes blank with the scent of our fucking mixed with the faint fragrance of her perfume. Lindsay is in the nonstop writhing and squirming mode beneath me with the pleasure my cock is providing her.

I'd gladly keep it inside her for hours to come, driving her insane with my thrusts. I feel her hand moving down over her belly and catch it before she can reach her target.

She glares at me with her dilated irises, flushed cheeks, and pouting lips. I can't help the amount of pride I feel for the beaten-up expression on her face. She's so ready to come, as if she was celibate for a long time.

Her orgasms should be mine and mine only, so I

slither my hand down to take over what she needs to get off. As soon as my thumb touches the moist flesh of her clit, she stills, digging her nails deep into my shoulders. She closes her eyes as tears roll down her temples. It doesn't take a rocket scientist to guess why she's crying.

Out of guilt.

But I see light shimmering at the end of the tunnel, because that guilt may be for the realization that I too belong in her heart.

Her hands are still rough on my shoulders, and her hips, surprisingly, are matching my thrusts. I wish she could mouth words of passion for me, moan my name, or just say anything. Instead, she keeps her mouth completely shut except for a few whimpers here and there.

My balls ache with the raw need to expel the boiling seed. I lower my head, burying my face in her hair, and thrust harder into her, until I explode and coat her insides with the evidence of my desire for her.

Something has to be said about coming inside a pussy without a condom. Even a man-whore like myself can feel the primal force of marking the woman as mine with my sperm.

I didn't come inside her the first time we had sex to have a reason to get her out of the living room so I could grab the video recorders without having her notice me. But now, after experiencing the ultimate pleasure of not having to pull out and finish the job with my bare hands, instead letting her pussy squeeze out the last of the drops, I curse myself for not having unloaded my shot inside her the first time too.

My cock remains hard despite emptying itself, so I continue rubbing her newly marked pussy muscles with slow and deep strokes to get my cream deeper inside her and to make her realize and come to terms with the fact that she's now mine.

I never thought I had any possessive tendencies, but knowing that she'll always carry a part of me with her, no matter who she ends up with, makes me want to beat on my chest with pride, like a caveman.

She doesn't push me away, but keeps on sobbing softly with a few moans here and there whenever I hit a deep spot. If I didn't know any better, I'd think her pussy is demanding another round of fuck. Maybe it does, but Lindsay would never give in to her pussy's needs. At least not now, and I have no desire to force on her more than she can handle.

Instead, I lower my head and let my lips touch hers, waiting for her to take over. Eventually her lips move and round mine, and I kiss her with all the emotions that are making my heart beat hard for her.

I don't blink an eye while our tongues rub each other and watch her expression change from sad to surprised, than back to sad again. Even her hands move up and wrap around my neck as our kiss deepens.

When I finally slide out of her body and roll down beside her, she snaps her eyes open and stares at me expectantly.

Rather than praising my skill of giving her two consecutive orgasms, as I'd have loved her to say, she sits up on the bed, crossing her arms around her chest and smashing her legs together, and puts up the same invisible barrier between us.

"Why did Michael hire me?" she asks, inflicting yet another pain into my heart with her question.

Has this been only about Michael and Ace? Has she not been even a tiny bit affected by our love-making? Has she used me? I finally feel how the women in my life must have felt at being used for my pleasure.

My chest constricts in pain as if stabbed over and over again by a sharp knife. It's definitely karma getting back at me for the heartbreaks I've caused.

Shall I continue feeding my ambition to win her heart? Or shall I move on to the next target?

When she repeats her question, I have no recourse but to explain everything to her; however, with the order of information I deem appropriate.

I try to smile to cover up the disappointment I have in her. "I'll tell it to you later."

"I don't accept that. Spill those beans now." She narrows her eyes at me with anger.

"I promise I'll tell you everything. But wouldn't you rather hear how I'll take Michael down?"

She frowns, perhaps considering her options, and then nods. "Okay. How exactly will you do that?"

"Frat House," I reply briefly.

"Frat House?"

I nod, straightening up, and jumping to my feet. As soon as I grab my phone, I dial Julie's number. "Start the plan now."

"Okay, boss," Julie says, and tingles of excitement course from the tip of my toes up to the top of my head.

Michael, start praying for your redemption now, because you might never get it if you're too late.

*

When one of the producers gave me an elevator pitch of Frat House over four years ago, I immediately knew it was what I'd been waiting for to destroy Michael.

"I received a fantastic screenplay. Imagine a cross-over of John Tucker Must Die and Sex and the City," Jared, my long-time friend and producer at Hawkins Media Group, said on a Monday morning. "But the catch is the main characters are four attractive college boys. They're all burned by the president of a sorority and set up a brotherhood to take their revenge by dating each and every girl in that sorority to turn them against the president. It's just the starting idea. We can modify it as you like; give each character a certain trait. Maybe make one of them a nerd, the other one a womanizer. Have one have a sister who has a crush on one of the characters to keep the story rolling. But my gut feeling is telling me to jump on it before someone else snaps it out of our hands."

I considered it within seconds as the elevator opened with a ding, and gave my answer. "I'm sold. We're going for it, but tell the screenplay writer that the contract will be on our terms."

I made sure the new TV series hit it big. I hired the actors myself, spent half a year hunting down the ten most talented, no-name actors whose looks could make a woman faint.

Then I hired another five-hundred women of varied ages, from twelve to sixty-five, to rate the attractiveness of the men I discovered. The top four received another half a year to get their acting skills top notch and their bodies in shape so that women nationwide would faint for them.

I, myself, shopped around for the most creative screenwriters and sat with them to improve the original draft, adding jokes and tear-jerking moments into the already brilliant plot.

Using my personal funds, I converted an unused set inside the Hawkins Media Studios into a college campus with all the classrooms, fraternity and sorority buildings, football fields. Nothing was insignificant enough to disregard.

Michael, who had never stood behind any of my ideas, was impressed by the developments and agreed to give the show the Thursday 9 p.m. time slot to compete with the rivaling sitcom of Hawkins Group Media's number one competition.

The pilot episode set a new record and garnered the largest audience of any series premier in the history of TV, only to quintuple the number at the final episode of the first season. I expected it to be popular, but so popular to rival the Super Bowl in terms of viewer numbers at the beginning of the next season, was insane.

The audience, most of whom are women, got crazier after each new episode, setting up fan blogs, and writing fan-fictions. #FratHouse became the constant hashtag for the trendiest topics on social media. Not to mention the millions of fans our blog and social media pages garnered.

Everyone was astounded by the amount of success the show gathered, but only the clever ones were quick enough to secure commercial slots from very early on. Money was coming in heaps. HMG stocks hit a record high.

Everything was a dream that would soon turn into a nightmare for Michael with just a word from me.

Early in the third season, I pushed the button for the next level of the game. Despite the wild fame of the series, I managed to manipulate the ratings it received, deliberately showing them getting lower after each episode, in order to show the HMG board members that the time to let it go was approaching.

Consisting of an elite group of white, old conservatives, the board members never really comprehended the reasons behind Frat House's wild success and easily warmed up to the idea of moving onto a more culturally appropriate show. I had to fake a phone call to keep myself from laughing in front of them at the ridiculous suggestions for the next big hit of HMG.

Before everything started, everyone on the team, from the cast to the screenwriters, was made to sign a contract stating they would follow my directions, even if it meant the premature death of the series.

I paid them generously so no one had to think twice to take the pen and scribble their signatures on the papers that would determine my future.

By the middle of the third season of the series, I slowly started spreading rumors about the cancelation of the series. If any of the board members had cared enough to check out Twitter, they would have been astounded by the level of fury and disappointment the recent tweets showed, and would never even consider killing the golden-egg-laying chicken, but they ignored the social media completely. So I pushed further and further, talking to big names in the industry about the company's plans to start something new, raising the premiums for advertising during the show to decrease the demand from interested businesses, and most importantly, preparing for my next position following the post-Frat-House HMG havoc.

Everything was working just as I planned, but what would determine if my efforts would hit or fail was the loyal fan base of the series. I recruited a team of twenty people to check the pulse of the audience and gave them a month to identify the top thousand craziest fans. Those precious jewels that live by Frat House almost day and night were invited to special celebrations to meet the actors, given gift cards, front-row show tickets, asked for their ideas for future episodes, in other words, bought and brainwashed. Through their help, I'll wreck HMG brick by brick with the intensity of a magnitude 9.0

earthquake.

*

Lindsay's chin is nearly touching her chest with shock as she listens to the filtered version of my plans. She barely moved for nearly half an hour during my talk, uncaring or having forgotten about her nudity and mine while lying down on the bed, facing me.

When her shock wears off enough for her to be able to talk, she asks with an angry expression on her face, "Is Frat House going to end?"

I have to laugh, really, because in the middle of all the troubles awaiting her, she has to ask that. Goes to show once more how successful the series has become. The fury on her face is the exact expression I want to picture on the rest of the audience, after they hear the news I'll announce very soon.

I just give my head a little shake, unwilling to share the rest of my plans. She lets out a loud breath of relief and rolls on her back, lacing her fingers right below her chest, her breasts poking seductively up in the air. Her legs are crossed, the tip of her foot occasionally touching my leg.

"That's a brilliant plan, but I still don't see how it'll stop Edward." She licks her lips, bringing out their deep shade of red, the sight of them making my cock stir.

Ignoring her question, I allow myself to move my hand over to her chest and cup one breast. Another wave of shock catches her off-guard and her eyes close instantly. I fucking hate having her close her eyes because of the possibility that she might be dreaming about that bastard touching her instead of me.

Her breasts are small but firm and the nipple is hard enough to slide through my fingers as I knead her breast. I slide to get closer to her and lean my head down to capture the needy nipple. My cock grows thicker at the sound of the soft moan escaping her mouth. She's not without interest and lets me suck on her nipple.

Just when I start to move my leg to slide it between her thighs, she clutches my chin and lifts my head up. "What about my contract with Michael? When are you going to tell me what he really wants from me?"

"I can't say anything about it until the time comes."

She jerks up, disappointment clear in the furrow of her eyebrows, and releases herself from my hold. I watch her jump off the bed and look for her clothes.

"Where are you going?" I ask, feeling cold without her body warming up the bed.

"To sleep. You didn't expect me to spend the night with you, did you?" Her tone is full of sarcasm and irritates my nerves. I want her submitting to me the way she was a few minutes ago.

"Come back here," I order, patting on the space she was lying on. "I'm not finished with you."

Ignoring my order, she slides her legs through her panties and pulls them up, without even caring about looking at me. My anger shoots up when she turns her back to me as she puts on her dress. WTF!

"Come back, I said."

As if I didn't say a word, she pulls up the zipper of her dress and straightens it around her hips. She tilts her head only enough for me to see her smirk and steps toward the door. Holding the door knob, she turns to face me.

"What will you do if I don't? Call off our deal? I didn't sleep with you out of desire, but out of necessity. If you don't hold up your end of your bargain, I'll go to Michael, offering to tell him all about your plans for his ruin in exchange for releasing Chloe, releasing me from my contract, and protecting Ace from Edward. How about that?" With that, she opens the door and bangs it closed as she leaves.

I punch in the pillows for my stupidity, but more so for misreading her signs. Didn't she enjoy the minutes I pleasured her at all? Was it all a silly illusion? Will she now go back to Ace and let him fuck her?

Fuck.

A smile of satisfaction spreads across my lips as I remember the video cameras hidden at the four corners of the suite. Ace must have watched my little performance with Lindsay. Even if she won't accept being mine, the memories of her squirming beneath me will follow Ace forever.

CH 3 - The Boycott

I rush out of the Summer Suite, running down the hall toward the stairs, and from there up to Ace's office. I have to find him and explain to him before he comes to the wrong conclusion. If there's one valuable thing that comes out of the decadent minutes I shared with Zane, it's that I now fully know I belong with Ace and no one else.

I still don't know how Zane will stop Edward from hurting Ace, but the piece of information Zane foolishly shared with me will give me a new chance to get out of this mess. Michael will be willing to do whatever I demand of him in exchange for hearing Zane's plots to ruin him. I hope it won't come to that, though. Zane has worked years waiting for the fruit of his plans. And Michael finally losing his power and money will serve him right after all he has done to the people close to him.

But if that information is what I'll need to use when nothing else works, I won't blink an eye to share it with Michael, especially to take revenge on Zane for forcing me to have sex with him in front of Ace.

My anger rises to the surface as I remember how Zane hovered over me and coerced my body into reactions I'd never willingly do in a thousand years. Traces of his saliva must be still coating my skin, and I don't want to even begin to think of his juices inside me. It'll take a series of hot showers to get rid of the residuals of him from my

28

body.

My heartbeats quicken as I reach Ace's office door. It's closed. I take the last step breathless and pained, trying to imagine how much he must have hurt. My hand doesn't move toward the door handle as I wish, despite the aching need to see him and hear his forgiveness.

I bite my lip and clutch at my purse as I try to regain my composure. I'll face him, although it'll be shameful to look in his eyes right after having sex with another man. I hate Zane for causing another mess for me to deal with.

What if, unbeknownst of my reasons for having sex with Zane, Ace indulges in another girl to take his revenge on me? What if he's fucking Laila behind this door, right now? Can I stomach it? Obviously not, but I'll have to overlook it and forgive him, as I hope he'll do the same for me.

Finally my hand obliges my mind's order and proceeds forward, cupping the handle firmly. I turn it and push the door, but it won't open as it's locked. I plaster my ear against it to catch any noise hinting at Ace's presence on the other side and wait several minutes in that position, to no avail. No sound comes.

Oh, God, where is he?

Hopelessly, I look around in the dark corridor for someone to come out and tell me where Ace is and that he's okay. What if Edward changed his plans about waiting for tomorrow after seeing Ace's reluctance in servicing him? Oh, please no. Anything but that.

I rush back to the stairs to go to the ground floor in an attempt to find someone. My muscles partially relax when I spot Nick with a group of three other young men.

"Nick," I call out and pace toward them. "Have you seen Ace? I need to talk to him."

"Oh, yes. A couple of minutes ago. He said he was

leaving and Alexander would be in charge 'til he comes back tomorrow. Would you want me to give him a call?"

"No, thank you. I'll call him on my cell." Breathing out my desperation loud enough for the boys to hear and look at me with curious eyes, I pull my phone out of my purse and walk toward a secluded corner for privacy.

Ace doesn't pick up my call, so I text him.

"Ace, please answer my call so we can talk. What you saw in the Summer Suite was for your benefit. I overheard your talk with Edward and asked Zane for help. Please, at least give me a chance to explain myself. I'm worried about you." I hesitate, and consider adding "I love you" at the end of the text, but dismiss the idea in the hopes of saving it for a more appropriate occasion.

When I get no response to my text after twenty minutes of internal struggle and self-disgust, I hop into my car and drive to Ace's apartment. I bite all my manicured nails while driving, but that doesn't ease any tension.

The miles seem to triple on my way to his home, and only red lights find me. I feel if I don't talk to him soon, terrible things will come.

My phone buzzes in my lap, startling me. A timely red light comes on, and I stop to read the text, my entire body on high alert.

"You're expected at breakfast at Pleasure Extraordinaire at 9 a.m. sharp. Put on the blue dress with white stripes, the navy blazer, and IMPORTANT: Manolo Blahniks..." The text continues with more nonsense about my outfit and makeup, which can only mean it's from Edrick. I can hardly focus on the letters through the disappointment blurring my eyes. I floor the gas pedal as the light turns green and drive down the empty road toward Ace's home.

By the time I'm in front of the door to his apartment, I'm exhausted and at the end of my nerves. I won't rest if I can't get to him and force him to give me a chance to explain myself, however hurt he must be.

I don't have the key to his apartment with me, thinking he and I would get back here together. I knock on his door, my heart beating faster and harder with each second the door remains closed. I try again, again, and again, until my knuckles throb with pain, but no one answers the door.

I collapse on my buttocks, leaning against the door, and retrieve my phone to call Ace. A loud sob shakes my body as the call goes to voice mail. He's avoiding me on purpose, ignoring my calls and hiding from me, perhaps to hurt me back or, hopefully, get some alone time to absorb it all. A faint voice inside me says, it's likely the former, and that's exactly what Zane wanted.

Wherever Ace is now, I don't have a way to find him unless he wants me to, and I have no frigging idea how I will go through the night without knowing how he is and if he will forgive me.

Tears flow down my cheeks in abundance; sobs shake my body. My mind is urging me not to give up. He must be somewhere and I can find him if I ask the right people about his whereabouts.

I dial Alexander, his assistant at Pleasure Extraordinaire. Ace must have told him where he'd be going or at least would take his call in case of an emergency.

"Hello, this is Alexander at Pleasure Extraordinaire. How may I assist you?"

"Alexander, this is Lindsay," I say hurriedly, expecting my name would ring some bells, but add my last name anyway. "Doheny. Lindsay Doheny. I can't find Ace

LIV BENNETT

anywhere. Could you please tell me where he is? It's very important that I see him."

"I'm sorry, Miss Doheny, but I received clear instructions from him not to inform anyone about where he is. I am sure he will contact you as soon as he is available."

"What does it mean as soon as he is available? Is he with someone else? Another woman?"

He remains silent at first only to end the stillness with, "I'm sorry, I can't be of any help to you tonight. Have a good night." Just like that he hangs up on me.

I listen to the dial tone awkwardly, my shock at his rudeness keeping me from acting. Once my senses return, I collect my purse and do the only thing I can in these circumstances and drive back to my home, the tiny apartment that hasn't hosted me for a week now.

After a quick shower and change into a t-shirt and shorts, I grab my phone and lie down on my bed, resting my head on my arm and staring at the screen of my phone.

An hour has passed without hearing from Ace. I've missed him so much. What will I do if he doesn't want me back?

Zane chose the worst possible way to get to me. Rather than ensuring the first step to a serious relationship with me, with his cruel move, he erased any sympathy I might have had for him, replacing it with white hot hatred.

Speak of the devil, a message from Zane buzzes my phone. "Check this out," it says, with a link to Twitter. I tap on the screen and tweets with the hashtag GetHMGDown fill my screen.

The top tweet, "WTF! It's official Michael Hawkins won't renew Frat House for the 4th season.

#GetHMGDown" has been retweeted more than a thousand times and been favorited three thousand times in a matter of, what, an hour or two? The figures will easily reach ten thousand by the morning.

I skim through the other tweets, most of which include curse words addressed to Michael or HMG.

Minutes turn to hours as I read through the hate-filled tweets, feeling gratitude for having something to distract my mind while waiting for the call or text from Ace that never comes. Finally, my body succumbs to the overwhelming stress of the day and relaxes into a nightmare-filled sleep.

The loud ringtone of the phone makes me jolt up in the bed. I grab the phone that slid down beneath my pillow in the night, but can barely open my swollen eyes wide enough to look at the screen of the phone. My nerves are on high alert with the possibility that Ace might be calling.

My hopes die in a matter of milliseconds as I read Edrick's name. I consider not answering it and going back to sleep, since he'll probably instruct me about my makeup style or make silly comments about the shoes I chose to wear yesterday. A loud yawning strikes me, but I tap on the screen to get the call.

"Lindsay, for God's sake, why don't you answer my calls?" Edward yells on the other side of the line.

"Sorry, I was sleeping." I wonder what time it is and turn to check the digital clock. It's only six fifteen.

"It's no time to sleep. You're expected at an urgent meeting with Michael."

I roll my eyes and mentally curse Edrick and Michael for waking me up from a deep sleep for something I'm sure is utterly stupid or abusive. Did the Russian minister get a painful hard-on that Michael wants me to take care

33

of? Then I remember Zane's plan and the hostile tweets against Michael and jump off the bed.

"Sure. Where is the meeting?" I ask as I pull my t-shirt over my head with my free hand.

"At the company headquarters. I'm sending Dan to pick you up."

"It's not necessary. I can drive myself."

"Don't argue with me. There's hell going on outside of the headquarters. Dan will drive you into the building through a secret entrance so you can arrive here safely."

I'm oddly touched by Edrick's care about my safety, but he's probably doing it out of duty and not necessarily out of concern for me.

"Sounds serious. What's going on?" I add, trying to sound both curious and worried to conceal my knowledge of Zane's plan.

"You'll find out when you get in. Dan will be in front of your apartment building in ten minutes. Don't make him wait." He hangs up.

I hurry to dial Ace, but he doesn't take my call, so I leave a message. "Ace, you don't want to talk to me, I understand, but just know that you're the only man in my mind and in my heart. And please, please be careful. Edward is planning to use his men to force you if you don't obey him."

I rush to the bathroom for the quickest shower I can ever remember having, and in exactly ten minutes I'm climbing into the company car Edrick sent for me, wearing a white silk blouse and a knee-length, black skirt. I greet Dan, who offers me a friendly "Good morning."

"Do you know what's going on?" I ask, taking advantage of his friendliness.

"A group of Frat House fans are attacking the building with eggs and tomatoes. I don't know exactly what caused the outrage, but I heard from the receptionist that an insider had leaked some sensitive information about Frat House, and that drove the fans mad." He slides onto the main street and heads toward Sherman Oaks, where Michael is waiting for me and probably the rest of his employees for the emergency meeting.

"Oh," I blurt out and look for my phone inside my purse to check the social media to get a better picture of the state of affairs.

It looks like no fan of Frat House has slept during the night because Twitter and Facebook are abuzz with the news of the cancelation of Frat House. The top trendiest tweets are all about Frat House, as if the world is spinning around Frat House. Michael Jackson's death probably garnered less attention than Frat House. According to Los Angeles Daily News, two main shareholders are planning to sell off their shares of Hawkins Media Group the first second they hear the opening bell of the NY Stock Exchange tomorrow. Goes to show how efficiently Zane planned every detail.

Remembering him makes my stomach roil in disgust. I hope I won't see him in the next two hundred years, but if Michael is ordering me, an insignificant employee in the marketing department, to attend an emergency meeting, he must have personally pulled Zane out of bed so he can find an immediate solution to the drama.

As Dan maneuvers to the avenue where HMG headquarters resides, I notice dozens of people with banners and grocery bags pouring onto the streets, pacing toward the direction we're heading.

Banners, I understand, but what's with the grocery bags? I try to get a glimpse of what's written on the banners and see Michael's name is the one common element on all. The closer we get, the more people crowd the sidewalks on each side, reaching into the hundreds, and oddly all are women.

A few yards away from the building, I realize the reason for the grocery bags as I see people smashing tomatoes and eggs onto the building walls. There are no police around to interfere. Is that also Zane's doing, or have the police not yet been informed about the protests?

The protestors scream their demands to have Frat House back on the air in unison and pour out their threats of tearing down the building if Michael doesn't comply with their wishes. Michael has forced his wishes upon his family and employees over the decades, now all his hostility is coming back at him to bite him in the ass. I can't exactly say I'm sorry for him.

Dan swings the car around and enters a small street, then another one, and from there through a tunnel, which I assume is the secret entrance to the headquarters. Two men in what I guess are bullet-proof uniforms usher me out and through the doors where I'm welcomed by Jen, the receptionist.

I notice Zane by the elevators with three other men I recognize from one of the marketing team meetings. Two are board members; the third is the head of HR.

Zane gives me a slight nod of his head in acknowledgement of my presence. My hands form fists as I note the twitch of his lips while his eyes roam over my body slow enough for others to realize and turn toward me.

My cheeks feel warm with embarrassment when I'm confronted with the narrowed eyes of the three men accompanying Zane. I utter a faint "Good morning," and scan around casually as I wait for the elevator to come.

The doors open with a ding and the three men step inside without waiting for me or Jen. Zane holds his hand toward the cab, signaling for me to go in first, then follows me inside. He stands annoyingly too close to me as someone pushes the button.

Zane leans even closer and whispers in my ear, "Hope you had a good night's sleep because today will be a long, hard day," emphasizing long and hard as if he's talking about something else.

I struggle to hide how pissed I am at his unabashed move and glance at Jen awkwardly. When the elevator stops at the floor of the general conference room and the doors open, I intend to step out, but Zane grabs my elbow to keep me inside the cab and waits for others to leave before pushing the stop button.

As soon as the doors close on us, he shoves me to the wall and launches himself on me. His hand pushes mine down to his crotch and circles my fingers around his hard-on that was pounding into me just yesterday. Oh, God, how could I allow that to happen?

"I don't have the slightest idea how my mind will focus on the day ahead if you don't do something about it." He seethes through his teeth, glaring down at me.

I cringe in disgust as his warm breath mixed with the spicy scent of his cologne hits my nose. "Zane... I—"

"Zane, I, what? Huh? You'll do as I say. I don't give a damn shit if you go ahead and tell on me. Michael won't believe you, and at this point it doesn't matter anyway. He's too deep in shit to save his ass. However you ... if you don't take care of this—" he pushes his hips against me, and I see anger flaring up in his eyes, "I won't be moving a finger to stop Edward from driving to Pleasure Extraordinaire."

Danger and hostility pour out of his words, and for the first time I feel fear in his presence. "Zane, please. I already did what you wanted."

"That you did well, but you see, it was yesterday and today is a new day. You might as well get used to servicing my cock from now on." His voice is menacing, his expression sinister.

I gulp, unable to tear my gaze away from his threatening eyes. At least my stomach is calm, contrary to how it felt with Zane's sexual advance yesterday, although the prospect of feeling his penis inside me again is a far cry from welcome.

"I heard your bastard boyfriend spent the night with one of his ex's." He pauses, perhaps to watch my reaction to his words, as they rip through my heart.

I shiver internally at the thought of Ace with another woman. He didn't give me a chance to explain and instead ran to the arms of another woman to console himself. I shouldn't be upset with him for acting without thinking, but I can't stop the feeling of jealousy piercing deeply into my heart.

"He's over you," Zane adds, his lips twitching up into a sly smile. "And you should come to accept it. Why not start your new life without that douchebag by sucking my cock?"

"Zane, please, I don't want it. You're not going to make me fall in love with you this way. It's actually just the opposite," I say with a gentle voice, in case he's doing this out of genuine affection for me and not just for some selfish reason, and watch as his lips are pursed in a line and his nostrils flare. He's not used to rejections, I see, so I go a level harder. "I think I'm in love with Ace already. I can't get physical with another man while loving him."

His eyes widen with shock at my confession, and for a moment I think he'll release me and give up on his stupid idea of trying to win my love. But my hopes evaporate as he places a hand over my shoulder, forces me down on my knees, and unzips his pants. Without bothering to unbutton them, he slides his raging cock out of the opening of his pants and pushes it into my face.

"You let me fuck you last night; you'll do it today, too. Suck my cock now, or your love might be sucking on Edward's cock while his men fuck him in the ass."

Nope, he doesn't have the tiniest bit of affection for me, but just plain old egoism. I swallow hard at the image of Ace abused by Edward and his men and glance up at Zane. "When all this is behind us, I'll make sure you hear from the police about your sexual abuse."

Ignoring my threat, Zane places his hand on the back of my head and drives his cock between my lips, right into the back my throat. I inhale a long, low breath and gather as much saliva as possible into my mouth to avoid any feeling of puking and start working on his cock.

He tastes salty but smells clean otherwise. My hands are firmly gripping his hips to control his moves, but he's plunging into my mouth with hard and long strokes as if it's my sex. I can try to fight against it and prolong the torture or do as he wants and get him out of my hair sooner.

"Yeah, baby. Let it fuck your mouth," he murmurs, fisting both his hands in my hair. "Pull up your skirt. Pull down your panties. Let me see your ass."

I reach down and slip the hem of my skirt above my waist and shove my panties down, feeling the cold air brushing against my buttocks. Zane growls above me. I risk a glare at him and see his expression twisting with lust and satisfaction as he stares at my reflection through the mirror.

"Push your ass back. Show me your pussy. I'm gonna fuck it hard."

I do as he says while bobbing my head up and down

on his cock, rolling my lips tightly against his shaft to make him come faster. He fights against it, but in a matter of a minute, he explodes into my mouth. His hands push my head against his hips to keep me in place so I have no chance to escape his seed jetting deep inside my throat.

I swallow quickly, barely breathing, my eyes moistening with the force of his still-hard cock hitting at the back of my throat.

"Lick it clean. Swallow my load." He watches me intently while my tongue swirls around the length of him, and then takes a step back, placing his now-flaccid cock inside his pants and zipping up.

"You know, I felt sorry for you last night and even a little guilty for having led you on those first days that I met you. But, now it's all gone. Vanished. I don't have the slightest positive feeling for you. In fact, I hate you," I say, as I get on my feet and pull my panties up.

"Watch your mouth or I'll fuck your ass in front of your colleagues."

When did he become such a despot? Perhaps he's always been and I noticed it only recently. Stupid me for having wasted feelings for him the first time we met.

Once we're both in a presentable condition, he pushes the button, and the doors open. Rather than heading to the conference room, he guides me toward his office.

"Michael is expecting us," I whisper, peeking up at him over my shoulder.

"He can wait all he wants. His minutes in this building are numbered." His eyes sweep up and down my body. "I'm not done with you, yet. There's one more hole I want to explore before the party starts."

A cold shiver crosses my body at the thought of Zane hurting me back there. He doesn't seem his usual calm self today, and might easily ignore my pleas to take it slow and instead easily cause damage.

Perhaps he's under the influence of alcohol or drugs making him act like a mad man; I can't be sure, but I should find a way to dissuade him before he goes ahead with his twisted desires.

Without giving me another opportunity to discuss it, he places his hand at the small of my back and guides me toward his office.

Opening the door to the ante-room of his office, we pass by the empty desk of his secretary and walk up to his office. My heart nearly flutters out of my chest as I notice Michael sitting at Zane's desk with a murderous look hardening his features, and I can't say I'm disappointed at seeing him, considering Zane's plans for me. Michael doesn't wait for Zane to close the door, and he leaps the distance between us and grabs Zane by the collar of his jacket.

"You motherfucker, you're behind all this, aren't you?" Michael growls with so much power I find myself running to the opposite end of the room with fear. Michael punches Zane's face, but keeps on holding his jacket so Zane can't avoid his assaults.

A part of me watches with satisfaction as pain surfaces on Zane's bleeding face, each drop of blood increasing the pleasure of seeing him suffer. He's deserved that and more.

"Yes, Father. It was me," Zane speaks through the punches. "I started planning your ruin years ago, and today is the day you'll finally pay for what you did to Mother. She killed herself because of you, you know that? She's gone because of your tortures. Now, see how much torture I'll give you while you watch the empire you built with your sweat and blood through the years, vanish into nothingness in a matter of days."

"Shut up." Michael throws his fist right at Zane's cheek, and Zane loses his balance, launches backward, and hits the door.

"Wait and see how much worse it'll get when I reveal all your illegal activities to the public. You'll rot in jail. Your inmates will line up in front of your cell to fuck your ass."

I curl behind the desk, hoping I won't be a target of these two uncaged wild animals. Michael launches forward, preparing for his next assault, but his phone rings, and he stops to look at the Caller ID. "Yes," he answers it with a loud, hostile tone. "What? Are you absolutely sure?" He turns abruptly in my direction, and I see his red face turning purple by the second.

For a moment, he stands still, staring at something on the wall, letting the phone slide down from his hand. The next second, he's lying down on the floor, his hand clutching at the tight collar of his shirt. He opens his mouth and fights for breath. I panic as I witness the color slowly draining out of his face.

Grabbing Michael's phone, Zane asks the caller what happened and listens with interest as the other person explains. He ends the talk with loud laughter that comes out more like the roar of a winning lion. "Someone leaked out all the contracts you made your fake girlfriends sign. As much as I hate to say it, it wasn't me, I appreciate the extra help from whoever it is that finally had the guts to reveal your true identity to the public. Now people will hate you for one more thing. No one likes to be lied to, especially year after year, like you did in front of millions. Admit it, you're gone. You're less worthy than dirt."

Zane kicks at Michael, who's already writhing in pain on the floor, choking, trying in vain to fill his lungs with air. Even though he's a monster, I can't find it in me to see him suffer as Zane throws forceful kicks one after another into Michael's stomach.

I finally have the courage to jump to my feet, running toward Zane, and push him away from Michael. When he's at a safe distance from Michael, I sink to my knees and begin unbuttoning Michael's shirt.

"I think he's having a heart attack," I yell in panic. My brain shuts down; my hands shake as my fingers work through the buttons of his shirt.

Zane comes back beside me, and I fear he'll send another kick into his father's fragile body. "Let him die. That's the best for everyone."

Maybe, but it can't be me who decides who should die or not. I can't carry the consequences of such an enormous decision on my shoulders. "No. Call 9-1-1. We need to save him."

Michael's eyes close. His body stops fighting, his hands relaxing heavily on mine. In utter shock, I stare at his lifeless face and realize yet another person is dying in my hands.

CH 4 - Michael the Great

I'm seconds away from landing at the pits of hell, and my own son wants to push me further down over the cliff. How have I ended up at this point? To what do I owe the honor of winding up with the pity of a strange girl, who might or might not convince my son to grant me my life back?

Ah, yes I know. To my heartless nature. To my egotistical needs. To my sadistic tastes. I wouldn't have known those pearls of words could be used for describing me until I heard them spilling out of the mouth of my own daughter, Chloe, the very reason for me continuing my never-ending fight to survive.

I avoided meeting her when she was born for fear of losing my mind over another helpless girl, my girl, and the terror of being unable to protect her from the ugliness that's called life.

But I couldn't escape it. The harder I tried, the stronger the pull became. And when I finally saw her and held her gaze that shimmered vulnerability at its worst, I knew life was offering me yet another stroke-inducing challenge.

Worse yet, she just had to look like my mother—a doomed woman who gave her last breath at the hands of barbarians.

Yes, the inevitable is starting. The milestones of my life start rolling before my eyes like a movie. The true happiness I felt as a child with my parents and younger sister, working on our farm, chasing after the chickens is the easiest to remember. Oh, the sweet lightness of being protected and not having to worry about a thing.

I'd look up at my father and admire his strength and determination to keep his family happy and provided for. My mother's infinite love for us always kept my heart warm.

Until one day, my father passed away after an accident, and my mother was left behind to care for my sister and me and our little farm.

Running a farm alone while raising a family in rural Pennsylvania wasn't the easiest of challenges in those early years of the sixties. So she asked for help from Jeffrey, the brother of my deceased father. Happily, he wanted to help her out, sometimes more than she bargained for.

Very soon, Jeffrey and his seventeen-year-old son began with their abuses. First it was the ever-decreasing harvest, the farm animals disappearing one by one to the so called burglars, then my sister's unusual hysteria attacks.

It all became clear Jeffrey and his son were selling off most of the harvest and animals behind my mother's back. Money could be a motivation to do stupid things like stealing, but what possible reason could justify raping a thirteen-year-old girl?

My innocent little sister was not only shattered after the death of our father, but also by being molested by those lowly creatures. They scared the life out of her, that's why she kept it as a secret for over half a year. Only when I witnessed what was going on with my own eyes, did she have the courage to open up to my mother and me, crying out her embarrassment and shame as if she had some fault in it, while she showed us her bruised body.

My mother loaded up the rifle and in the middle of the night banged the door of their home open. Jeffrey came down in his dirty pajamas, smirking at my mother's attempt to bring justice to the world. Jeffrey Jr. sneaked behind me and grasped my arms behind me while holding his gun to my temple.

His father quickly captured my mother, throwing her rifle to the floor, and stripped her naked from the waist down and, before my own eyes, raped her like the animal he was. My mother turned her face to the other side and held all her screams caged inside her, didn't even make a sound of her pain while I struggled to escape Jeffrey Jr.'s grip.

I threw up, couldn't look anymore as Jeffrey pulled up his pajamas, lit a cigarette, and ordered his son to continue where he'd left off. Jeffrey Jr. tied my hands with a rope before taking his father's place.

The two took turns raping my mother while in between damaging her fragile body with repeated punches and kicks. They went on with their barbarity even when my mother stopped moving, lying lifelessly on the floor, with blood and dirt covering her entire body.

I cried. I cried out so much that night, I could cry no more for the rest of my life. When Jeffrey finally announced that they were done, he ordered his son to untie me.

Holding up my mother's rifle at me, my dear uncle told me that I had only one minute to run as fast as I could and get the fuck out of town or he'd come and do the same thing to my sister. Despite the horror I'd just witnessed, I spun around on my feet and stormed out through the empty field fast, so at least I could spare my sister the pain.

It took only fifteen minutes to get the most necessary belongings gathered up in a suitcase and run for the bus. We didn't have any other relatives to ask for help. The only relative I heard of was my mother's sister in San Diego.

After days of traveling, we arrived in San Diego with heartache, but also a little hope to forget the pain. Yet, the unfortunate events didn't stop hovering over us. We found out that our aunt had passed away two weeks before.

Nowhere to go and with a little cash that would last only a few days, we took shelter in a roadside motel in Escondido. It was where I met my future wife, the good-hearted and beautiful Irene.

Only through her help, her father, the owner of the motel, offered me a job as the toilet cleaner until his real housekeeper was recovered from whatever illness she was suffering from.

Irene worked in a bakery in downtown Escondido and, again, helped my sister get a job as the dishwasher there. I wasn't entirely sure why she was being so generous to us, but I had a hint, and each day that hint got closer to conviction.

She was interested in me in a romantic way. Everyone in town loved her and continued flocking to the little bakery where she worked, despite the less than stellar pastries they provided. I wasn't immune to her contagious smile and big heart either, although I was aware of my sexual tendencies even at that tender age of sixteen, and spoiled her with flowers and chocolates.

She saw through me, understood that I loved men, but proudly wore the engagement ring I bought for her years later, then took my name, and bore my children.

If there was ever a woman I could imagine myself being married to, it'd be Irene. Only Irene.

My homosexuality wasn't the only hurdle hindering Irene from being with me in those early days of our friendship. She was engaged to the son of the bakery owner.

Edward Neuberger.

One glance at him and I knew he shared my likings, not that I was expert at anything regarding my likings. As soon as we had the confessions behind us, Edward and I entered a long journey of personal and sexual discoveries. He could make me forget about my past and I could make him forget about his loneliness. We promised each other an eternal bond and a future where both of us held the ultimate power.

I was determined I'd save every penny that wasn't used for food or shelter and use every opportunity to multiply it. In a matter of three years, I owned a radio station, an apartment, and a car. That was an accomplishment I could never have dreamed of as a farmer's son in rural Pennsylvania. I enrolled my sister in a catholic school for girls and married Irene. However, the tragedy of my mother burned in hot flames in my heart.

One fine night, I decided I couldn't take it anymore and drove back to my hometown in Pennsylvania with two well-built men to assist me in my pursuit for justice. Jeffrey and his son had spread their claws all around the land my father had left for us, behaving as if they owned it.

I was going to hand them to the police after I had my two men roughen them up, but when I found out what they did to my mother, my original plan was quickly forgotten.

Rather than burying her in our family graveyard, they'd

chopped my mother's body into small pieces and fed them to the pigs to get rid of the evidence of their crimes. Jeffrey explained the excruciating details, flashing his yellow teeth at me shamelessly, as if he was telling a joke and not the horror of my mother's end.

I did the only thing I could do to keep myself sane. My two men tied them up while I went through the toolbox to find a rusted saw. Both Jeffrey and his son's eyes grew large in panic, looking as if they'd pop out of their sockets as they realized what I had in mind as a suitable punishment for them.

I didn't blink as I slashed Jeffrey's hand. He passed out with pain, but I made him sniff alcohol to awaken him for more torture. I felt alive, seeing the horror filling Jeffrey Jr.'s face when I was finished chopping his father's hands and feet.

I moved on to Jeffrey Jr. while my men covered Jeffrey's arms and legs with sticks and cloths to stop the blood from flowing. I wanted them suffering, not dead. They'd continue living in misery without their body parts until I decided it was time for them to die.

However, I couldn't just leave them like that. I ordered my men to find the filthiest man in town—filthiest in terms of morality—and hired him on the spot as the personal caretaker of Jeffrey and his son.

He'd be paid a good amount of salary if he raped both men in their asses every day twice a day. He told me he'd have done it for free; that's how filthy he was. He'd also be responsible for their food and general hygiene. The amount of care he'd give to them was up to him. As long as they didn't die, I didn't care how callous he was with his subjects. The longer my uncle and cousin lived and got their daily potions of sperm flushed into their assholes, the more money I promised my new, filthy employee.

Together with my two men, I watched in complete joy the first round of their asses being raped. Although receiving it daily still didn't feel a sufficient punishment for what they did to my family, I was running out of time and they looked utterly miserable and in pain to the point of unable to make a sound as they cried and begged for my mercy.

At the end of the show, I paid my personal torturer his first payment with the promise of more and informed him about my future surprise visits to evaluate the quality of the work he was expected to deliver.

Nobody can cross Michael Hawkins without receiving a fitting punishment. Nobody.

*

I feel hands grabbing me by my shoulders and my body shakes. Cold fingers curl around my chin and nose, and warm breath is forced into my lungs. Low murmurs of my son remind me of the last seconds before I collapsed onto the floor. The excruciating pain I had right before everything turned black returns in harsh waves, yet, I don't even have the strength to groan out the pain.

"Enough, Lindsay," Zane yells. "Let him die." The hands and warm breath leave my body all of a sudden.

"Let me go, you fucking idiot. He's your father. Have some respect for life," Lindsay screams. I hear heavy breathing and more screams. They must be fighting. Then I hear Zane growl like a hurt animal followed by a thud on the floor. No sooner than his curses commence, I feel Lindsay sit beside my body and the cold fingers resume their positions on my face.

"You should have kicked him in the balls," Lindsay says, I guess, to me. "You'd think men would know their weak points, but no. In 99 out of 100 cases, it's women who use this technique to paralyze men," she murmurs and I realize she must have stopped Zane with an assault to his crotch. Pride swells my chest, along with the warm breath of Lindsay entering my lungs.

Between the mouth-to-mouth resuscitation, she continues shaking my body together with occasional slaps on my cheeks. I'm not sure if the slaps really belong to CPR, but hey, at least she's trying.

"Open your eyes, Michael. Your time hasn't come yet. I won't allow another person to die in my hands. Do you hear me? You're not dying today. You'll wake up and save Ace from your sick boyfriend. Do you hear me? Edward is after Ace. He's planning to rape him today. Now wake up and save your son for fuck's sake. Wake up!"

More than the slaps I'm being exposed to, it's her words that breathe the life back into my limbs and pump blood into my heart. Edward, my lover, wants my son in the most corrupt way? Anger storms into my veins, shaking my body more than Lindsay's small hands, and my eyes flutter open.

"Fuck, he's back," Zane growls and shoves another kick into my ribcage. I'm not sure what hurts more; his kick or his intense desire to see me dead.

Lindsay jumps up on her feet and digs her fingers into Zane's crotch. That move seems to have the effect of a bullet in the chest for Zane, because he doubles over in pain and lets out an embarrassing cry.

"I'll castrate you on the spot if you so much as touch him again." Lindsay keeps her hand between Zane's legs a little longer before turning her attention back to me. Honestly, if I survive today, I'll hire her as my personal bodyguard.

While Zane yells out his cat-like moans of pain, Lindsay leans over me, her face only inches away from mine. "Don't think I like you even the tiniest bit," she whispers. "But, I can't for the life of me allow a person to die, even someone I hate with all my being. But in exchange for my favor, you're going to leave my sister, Chloe, Ace, and me alone. Do you understand me? If you agree to that, I'll call 9-1-1 and get help for you." She stares at me, waiting for my response.

I try to give my head a nod, but immense pain stops my efforts. Instead, I blink my acceptance.

"Is that a yes? Did you blink to say yes?"

I blink again and try one more time to nod my head. This time it works or at least a little bit.

Placing a hand on my heart, she reaches for the phone on Zane's desk with her other hand, dials, what I assume is 911, and gives information on my health and the address of the office in an oddly calm manner, all the while staring directly into my eyes. I haven't had someone genuinely care for my health since Irene.

Shame clutches her ugly hands around my heart, piercing pain on each side for the dreadful plans I had for Lindsay and her sister.

"You're making a huge mistake." Zane appears behind Lindsay, not sparing a glance at my side. "He doesn't deserve to live."

"Look who's talking. At least he didn't force me to suck his stinky dick," Lindsay replies back, shooting a scary look of anger at him.

I close my eyes to stop myself from exposing myself to more shame. I can't say I'm proud of how my only biological son turned out to be, though I shouldn't be surprised. And deep down, I know none of this is his fault. It's me, as his father, to be blamed for everything. He just followed his father's footsteps.

"Michael," Lindsay cries in panic and I snap my eyes

open again. She lets out a loud breath of relief as she sees I'm not dead. After a long moment of staring at me, she asks, "Is Chloe okay? Did you hurt her?"

This time I can't hold her gaze and use the last drops of energy I have to look away. Chloe is fine, if fine means she's alive.

She's my biggest mistake as a father. I'd much rather be a father to a dozen sons, but being a father to a girl is much harder than anything else I took upon myself in my life. Not a day has passed that I didn't fear she, too, would experience a horrible rape, just as my mother and sister did.

Men are corrupt. Most of them are. To protect her, I had to force hard standards into her life, but that fear ate me from the inside out, and more often than not, revealed my evil face to her.

As if confirming my deepest anxiety, Chloe had to get engaged to Dylan Berenson, whose one and only motivation is to get back at me for being the new owner of his father's country club. He'll chew her up and spit her out the minute he takes his revenge on me.

Lindsay grasps my chin to turn my face to her and glares at me, but with concern in her eyes. "You're a piece of shit. You know that, don't you? What kind of father pulls that kind of shit on his own kids?"

Paramedics arrive, saving me from both another cardiac arrest and Lindsay's hurtful comments. Three men hover over me, connecting my arms to cables, covering my mouth with an oxygen mask under Lindsay and Zane's curious stares, and usher me out.

Just before we leave, I glance at Lindsay one last time, unable to believe thanks to her I might get a chance to continue living. She doesn't hold my gaze and instead turns to Zane and asks, "Tell me now why Michael hired me, or I swear on my dead niece's grave I'll report to the police everything you did to Michael and me."

"Uranium," Zane responds, sending me one last loathing glance before my eyes close and blankness takes over everything.

*

Money makes the world spin. When I worked as the toilet cleaner at the motel Irene's father owned, I thought I'd be completely satisfied if I had a home of my own and a steady job that paid the bills. That notion changed when I started earning money—the kind of money that could pay for a high-end, handmade Italian suit and fine leather shoes to go with it.

I wanted more, and the more money my bank account hosted, the poorer I felt compared to all the money I could make.

When I made my first million, I didn't take my wife to a fancy restaurant to celebrate the milestone—far from it. I sat at my desk to draw out a plan to double my fortune. I felt small, insignificant, compared to the really powerful businessmen. They looked down on me with pity, the way I wrinkled my nose at people with less money than I had.

The real powers, if they wanted, could erase me in an instant. I could be wiping up toilet bowls before I could grasp what they had done to me.

And my sister?

How could I protect her from the evils of the world without money backing me up?

That fear kept me sleepless at night and made me work most of my waking hours so I could sit on a solid foundation. One day, maybe. Even when I crossed the line of five hundred million, my fortune could never suffice to give me the calm I yearned for.

There were enough billionaires in the world that could

crush me with the blink of an eye. The mansions and the cars I possessed could change hands faster than I could think it. I wasn't powerful enough to withstand and be myself. Even Henry Ford, the grand genius and pioneer businessman, as wealthy as he was, couldn't stand behind his ideas against Jews, and had to take a step back and apologize to them for his anti-Semitic ideas in order to save his declining business.

I wanted to reside on a level of power where no matter what I did or said I'd remain indestructible. Was that kind of power possible? I believed so, especially because of my unbreakable bond with Edward, who was taking his chances and succeeding at an impeccable career in politics.

The good thing about having a lot of money is that you can easily make more money with it. Well, if you're smart, of course. You'll have more room for the risky opportunities, and usually the higher the risk involved in a project, the more money you can expect to make.

When Edward informed me about a secret governmental investigation going on about Berenson's Country Club, I knew I had to dive right in and invest half of my money so I could double my entire fortune and become a billionaire. It was a one-time venture, and only I could achieve it.

The Berenson's Country Club had large reserves of uranium, of a grade suitable for use in the manufacture nuclear weapons.

One day, back when I was still struggling to make my first million, a very wealthy and well-meaning businessman told me over a joke, "If you want to be rich, go into the medical or weapons industry. Those two are sure ways to fill up your pockets."

Over the years, I mentally kicked my own ass for not

listening to him and having ended up in media, where I could easily be targeted and taken down. Remembering his words, I used all my influence to get my hands on the land in question. Better late than never, although my move earned me more enemies.

I could convert most of the country club into residential homes and sell them for a decent price as a cover-up project for the real money-making machine that was the uranium brewing beneath the surface.

Soon as the word about high-quality uranium started spreading around in the international arenas, the offers began pouring in. Iran. Saudi Arabia. China. North Korea. Russia.

I was flying on cloud nine for the attention my new, secret endeavor received and for the amount of money my willing, soon-to-be associates were ready to put on the table. By the end of the deal, I would easily land on the billionaire's list.

I decided to choose Russia as my buyer, since they also had the technology and knowhow to extract uranium, saving me from the hurdle and the risk of looking for qualified employees who might or might not keep their mouths shut regarding the secrecy of the project.

Everything was going according to plan. I hired Edelman Construction to deal with the cover-up construction of the residential homes while a group of Russian-engineers, handpicked by Devora Vasilyev herself, ran the uranium extraction, away from curious eyes.

I even managed to deceive a Saudi Arabian Sheik, promising him my top-quality uranium with the condition of getting half of the money before the shipment as a deposit. That fool must be beside himself with his anger at losing that amount of money, and he can't even ask for help to avenge me for fear of being ridiculed for getting into such a ludicrous deal.

Everything was great until Edrick conveyed to me the news that three construction workers at the site had developed cancer. One thyroid, one leukemia, and one in the kidney.

I showed him the reports of the World Health Organization that stated uranium had no adverse health effects whatsoever on humans. He probably believed them. But, he's just one person and works for me. What about the millions of people who only see three men suffering from cancer and who also happened to work beside a uranium mine? I had to make sure the word about that little datum didn't get out.

However, my hands were tied when the news that could literally destroy my life's work came to my attention.

I clearly remember that afternoon when I was having a friendly chat with Tiffany Jordan, my then girlfriend-on-paper, in a hotel suite in New York. She had a pleasant personality and spoke joyously as if we were long-time friends coming together for an afternoon of chit-chat.

My phone rang, and she nodded with an amicable smile and retired to the bedroom assigned for her. A feeling of discomfort struck me as I tapped on the screen of my phone, although I had no idea of what was coming.

"Boss, Michael, you have to hear this," Edrick shouted at the phone.

I wanted to remind him to keep his respect for me at all times, but something inside me stopped me from punishing him for his outrage and let him speak out whatever it was that was causing him this disrespect.

"What is it?" I asked rather calmly although every inch of me was aware something big was coming.

"Taylor Garnett gave birth to a stillborn malformed child."

Taylor Garnett, the director of my construction project on the Berenson's Country Club, right next door to the uranium mine.

I felt the blood abandoning my body. My heart seemed to have stopped. I could neither breathe nor move. The room turned dark, and in the middle of that darkness, I saw my sister and Chloe being raped and I had to watch them helplessly, just like I had during the last hours of my mother's life.

Taylor Garnett wasn't a poor construction worker who could easily be bought with a little money and a promise of the education for his children. She had millions, hence possessed a certain amount of power.

"But that's not all," Edrick added. "The birth was videotaped and is now all over YouTube."

Dear goodness, could it get any worse? This news had the power to turn everything upside down for me and my family. It wasn't just words, but visuals. The public would go crazy if they found out the malformation of Taylor Garnett's child could be related to the frequent exposure to uranium.

My enemies had been waiting for an opportunity like this and would savor it by attacking me on the spot. When you climb a ladder to a very high point, like me, the number of haters will grow, as well as the magnitude of their hatred for you. Then one can only imagine the amount of damage they could cause.

I didn't wish to expose my children and my sister to any kind of malice, much less from those jealous losers who couldn't attain any success even if it was given to them on a silver plate. I had to control this.

Fortunately, I had the means to take down the video

before it got caught in the media frenzy. However, someone sneaked around and put the video back on YouTube two months later, and I'm positive it was Zane who was behind the comeback of the video.

The second time, however, I was too late to do anything about it. But at least I used those two months to do an intense research of Taylor Garnett's family. She and her husband were among the rare people who were honest and genuinely kind. And, well, generous, too. If donating most of one's fortune to free health clinics doesn't count as generous, I don't know what does. As angelic as Taylor Garnett might be, she had to be stopped, or at least controlled to diminish her potential destructive power on me.

I'm a firm believer in the idea that every problem has a solution, and the solution to my problem was delivered to me on a silver plate long before the problem with the malformed baby arose. Lindsay Doheny, Taylor's sister, would be the key to control Taylor's potentially dangerous moves. I had to provide Lindsay a deal so sweet she wouldn't have the will to turn it down.

Everyone has a weak point. If you want to control someone, you should discover his weakness and find a way to use it against him. Lindsay spared me the time and blurted out her weakness to me in our first meeting.

Sex.

Seeing the silver lining through the dark clouds, I immediately offered her the golden ticket to have as much sex as she wanted at an exclusive men's brothel, Pleasure Extraordinaire.

If the day came that Taylor Garnett found out about my secret uranium mine and wanted to sue me for causing her child's malformation, I could blackmail her with spreading the information about her sister's indecent visits to a sex club. I had almost no doubt a woman of Taylor's caliber would go to great lengths to protect her family's dignity and keep quiet even if it meant justice wouldn't take place.

Luck was on my side. The safety of my uranium mine was instantly secured when I found a sex tape of Lindsay with Zane. Lindsay was ready to accept anything I asked of her for once she realized the contract wasn't a joke, and I would do with her and her sister as I pleased. She became my backup plan if the worst-case scenario played out—she and her little sexual escapade.

How could I know the video was originally recorded to be made public and losing her dignity in front of millions wasn't a fear big enough for Lindsay to shut up?

I had to move a step ahead and push her limits to keep her under control. If she didn't care about herself, she'd most likely care about her lover's sister, Chloe? As much as it pained me to have to kidnap my own daughter, it was, after all, for her own good.

Everything I did until this date was for her and my sister so they both could live a life where men couldn't take advantage of them. Money was the only way to ensure men couldn't get their claws into them.

*

I hear a beep through my mad thoughts and a rush of sensation overloads my mind. Cold, warm, smell of chemicals, low murmurs. I have no idea how long I was gone. It could be days or mere hours.

I try to pay attention to the sounds to decide if I should open my eyes or not. If it's the police, I'll pretend to be in a coma forever to keep my secrets. If it's Zane, however, I'll gladly show him I'm not that easy to be rid of.

It's neither of my guesses. A soft, familiar female voice

hums close to my ear.

"I know you can hear me somewhere in there," says my little sister, whom I haven't seen for ages.

After high school, she enrolled in college to become a registered nurse under a different last name and led a low-key life away from all the glamour and wealth I could have given to her. It was better that way. The fewer people who knew about her, the fewer chances she'd have of getting hurt because of me.

However, that didn't mean I didn't spoil her with money and everything money could buy. She lived in a mansion I bought for her in San Francisco and has been working for the Red Cross as a volunteer nurse, taking care of the less-privileged individuals ever since, even using the home I bought for her as a shelter for women.

My hands shake at the possibility one of my enemies will recognize her as my sister and try to attack her in the worst possible way. She has to leave right now and continue with her life away from the public eye.

"You've caused enough pain," she whispers in my ear. "You're causing more pain now that you're about to die. Who'll protect me if you're gone? Who'll be at my side when there's danger?"

She's using my weakest point to get me where she wants me. She's my sister after all.

I open my eyes instinctively and glance at the face I haven't seen in nearly thirty years. The wrinkles on her oval face and the silver drops on her brown hair make her look like a stranger, but those shimmering blue eyes? The carbon copy of our mother's. And seeing them takes me back to the night when she was raped to death.

"The time has come to let go." A shy smile appears on her lips along with a tear rolling down her cheek. "You have to forget the past and forgive them."

Them? She can't be talking about them, can she? How can I ever forgive the two beasts who robbed us of our mother and our childhood? She sits in silence, waiting for me to take over the conversation, but I keep quiet.

"The doctors say you have a tumor in your lungs and that you have very little time left. Why didn't you tell me?" Her eyes skim around, more tears flushing down her cheeks. She blows her nose with a tissue and sighs softly. "How many years have passed? Thirty? Forty? They must have learned their lessons by now. Keeping on torturing them won't bring our mother back. But, if you release them, you'll have a chance to die in peace. I'll be with you. I won't leave you alone for a second. We'll spend our last days together. You, and me, and our memories of those good, old days with our mom and dad."

My eyes burn, and as miraculous as it might sound, a tear forms and slithers out of my eye, followed by others. After over forty years of drought in my eyes, now, for the first time, I'm crying like a baby.

Yes, I am dying. And yes, I'm lonely.

The very people I dedicated my life to don't even care enough for me to be at my side during my last days, except for my sister. It's painful to look back at my adult years and not find a single day where I was truly happy. It makes me wonder if nothing I did was right.

CH 5 - The Beginning of the End

Michael didn't die, however a small, but significant, part of me whispers I made a mistake by saving his life. As Zane delves deeper into his explanation about the uranium mine behind Michael's motivation to hire me, I feel less and less convinced about my decision for having called 911 to save him.

While I drive to the hospital to check up on Michael, Zane helps feed that doubting part in me by striking fear into my heart about Edward and his obsession with Ace.

As I drive through the underground parking lot of the hospital, I note several network vans parked alongside the street and dozens of reporters camping out near the hospital doors.

Seems like all hell has broken loose as the word about Michael's heart attack has hit the news, and now everyone wants a piece of information regarding Michael and HMG's future. Zane and I could barely make it inside the hospital through the sea of reporters, draining us with questions that I had no answer to.

A hospital aide guides us to the waiting room and instructs us to wait for a Dr. McBrine. While waiting, my eyes never leave my phone in the hope that Ace might call, and each time I sigh with disappointment, Zane narrows his eyes at me and shakes his head.

The digital clock on the screen reads 10:57. Where is Ace? I doubt he'll care enough for Michael to visit him at the hospital. Edward's absence from his lover's side can only hint at terrible things. I can't even begin to think about Chloe. Michael should finally open his eyes and tell us where he's keeping Chloe captive so at least we can get her to safety.

I stand on my feet, unable to keep calm enough to remain seated. Everything is so close to being resolved, but not quite there. It's unnerving and draining me of my resources.

We still haven't found Chloe. I still don't know if Ace is safe from Edward's evil desires. And I may or may not get Ace back as my lover. My stomach turns a little when I think about how he must have spent last night, possibly in the arms of another woman.

The only good news comes when Zane receives a phone call from Julie about the failure in the uranium delivery thanks to an anonymous tip-off to police, which I assume was either Zane or one of his people.

According to Julie, the police rushed in just before the uranium changed hands, but Devora and her husband could have escaped and possibly have already left for Russia.

"What are we going to do about Chloe?" I ask Zane, who's also standing beside me. "Edward might hurt her, or maybe Michael's men, if they find out he's now terminally sick. Why didn't you try to locate her rather than using up all your energy to ruin HMG?"

Zane breathes out loudly and leans against the wall, his arms crossed around his chest. I have mixed feelings about him. As much as I want him behind bars for molesting me, I'm also grateful for his meticulous plan to end Michael's reign.

Michael wanted to have me as his pretend girlfriend in order to silence my sister if she wanted to blame him for her malformed child. It's still beyond my comprehension how, rather than feeling guilty for causing such a major heartache to a family, Michael wanted to inflict more pain on Taylor by using me.

Exactly for that gratitude, I'll keep quiet about Zane's assault on me and on Michael, which led to his heart attack.

A middle-aged doctor, perhaps in her early forties, arrives with a serious frown on her face and introduces herself as Dr. McBrine. "We've stabilized Mr. Hawkins' vitals and expect him to recover from the heart attack without any apparent damage to major organs. That being said, the tumor in his lungs has grown drastically since the last time he was tested. He has only weeks left to live, if not days. I'm very sorry. At this point, nothing can be done about the tumor."

"Wait a second," Zane chimes in. "He has a lung tumor? Did I hear you right?"

"Yes, I thought you knew. I'm very sorry if I came across as insensitive about it. According to our hospital records, his tumor was detected a little over two months ago. However Mr. Hawkins didn't initiate any therapy at that time and said he wanted time to decide what to do about it. Unfortunately, the tumor grew much faster than Mr. Hawkins' oncologist originally estimated. This is the phone number of the oncologist if you want to get more details of Mr. Hawkins' condition, but at this point, there's really not much left to do to save him."

With my jaw dropped, I watch the doctor give a piece of paper to Zane, together with the contact information of Michael's oncologist. After informing us that Michael is now awake and we can visit him, Dr. McBrine walks back through the doors she came from.

Michael had a short life left, yet continued pushing

forward his plans about uranium. Was it his greed that motivated him until the last minute? Or perhaps he didn't think of himself as a fragile being, vulnerable to viruses and tumors, just like the rest of us. That'd fit very well into his 'I'm the super power. I'm God,' attitude. Whatever it is, he's receiving exactly what he deserves.

I have absolutely no doubt the tumor in his lungs is rooted to his exposure to uranium, just as was my innocent niece's fatal malformation.

I glance at Zane to see sadness dominating his features and pat him on his shoulder, gently. Thinking he must be sad that he's going to lose his father, I gather up the courage to ask him, "How do you feel about the news?"

"I'm shocked," he says, with half-hearted laughter, widening his eyes. "I spent the last four years planning for his destruction. If I knew he, himself, would cause his own end..." He throws his hands up in the air, I guess, over the lost time. "Looks I just wrecked the company I'm now about to inherit. That's a big bite to swallow."

Just when I start thinking Zane might have a little bit of humanity left in him, he disappoints me yet again with another selfish remark, but I don't have the right to be mad at him. It's Michael we're talking about; and I shouldn't blame Zane for feeling happy about the numbered days Michael has left to live.

"Let's go see him." I start walking toward the door Dr. McBrine left through and Zane follows suit with an annoying grin on his face.

In Michael's room, a middle-aged woman with fair, brown hair and sparkling blue eyes, wearing a blue silk blouse and black slacks welcomes us and walks up to Zane to hug him. From the curiosity on Zane's face, I realize he doesn't know her.

"Aunt Matilda? Is that you? I thought you were dead."

Zane embraces her, wrapping his long arms around her waist.

"That's what Michael wanted everyone to believe to protect me." Her voice trembles and tears stream down her cheeks. She pulls back, smiling through her sadness, and looks him up and down. "Look at you; you're a grown man now. Last time I saw you, you could barely walk."

I look away to give them some privacy and turn my gaze to Michael, who's staring back at me with tired eyes. He looks like a completely different person, spent and helpless with no traces of maliciousness on his face, and for some utterly strange reason, I find myself smiling at him.

"I'm very sorry," he mumbles the words out with long breaks as if it's causing him a great deal of effort. "Although I know it's useless to say. I can't...I can't bring back the past."

Zane and his aunt turn toward Michael, both looking curious at what he'll say next.

"I wish things were different." A loud cough interrupts Michael's words. When the coughing attack ends, Michael turns to Zane. "I wish I'd accepted your mother's request and gone to therapy years ago."

"Yeah, you should have." Zane nods, his face stern and unforgiving. "Maybe she wouldn't have killed herself then, and you'd have children who loved you, not hated you like Chloe and I do." It's funny how he doesn't include Ace among Michael's children.

"That's not the thing to say in this situation," Matilda cuts him off before he can shoot more words of hatred to Michael.

Zane sends his aunt a pained smile and untangles his arms from around her, taking a step back. "He kidnapped

Chloe. Did you know that?" Pointing his finger at me, he says, "He kidnapped his own daughter to control this girl, so her sister won't send him to jail for causing her to lose her baby due to the radiation his secret uranium mine caused."

Matilda's jaw drops in shock, and her hands reach up to cover her mouth. She looks as if she's restraining herself from firing away curse words.

Zane leaps and launches his hands on Michael's shirt. "Now, speak. Where are you hiding my sister? If you so much as touched her, I'll cut your throat right now."

Both Matilda and I rush toward Zane to grab his arms before he can hurt Michael. The machine goes off and loud beeps fill the room along with the ear-grating sounds coming from Michael's throat as he coughs.

A nurse storms inside and orders us out. When Zane doesn't obey, she informs the security with her phone. While Matilda and I try to pull Zane toward the exit, I hear Michael whispering, "Chloe is in the Mirror Mansion in Glendale."

Zane stops fighting and freezes on the spot, then yells, "You're not lying, are you? You wouldn't play your dirty tricks on me to take your revenge, would you?"

Michael shakes his head, writhing in pain as the coughing attack gets the best of him by the second. As the nurse hurries to cover Michael's mouth with an oxygen mask, Zane rushes out to the hall.

I stay paralyzed for a moment, trying to decide what I should do. Waiting here to see if Michael will come out of his coughing fit doesn't seem as vital as going after Zane to make sure Chloe is all right, so I hurry out and catch Zane as he steps into the elevator to the underground parking lot.

I let him drive my Audi because he knows the way

better than my navigator's descriptions and in a half hour we are in front of a majestic mansion. Is this the place Michael has been keeping Chloe captive? Even their prisons are nothing short of luxurious.

Two men at the gate try to stop us, but as soon as they hear Michael is in the hospital, fighting against death and realize that their next boss in line is Zane, they let him in and even walk him to the room where Chloe is being held.

To my ultimate relief, Chloe doesn't look hurt, at least not physically, although we find her with her hands and legs tied with thick ropes. She lets out a cry of joy and shock as Zane and I burst into the room.

Faint bruises on her face confirm what Ace told me about Michael's outrage the night before her kidnapping and makes me regret the compassion I felt for Michael when I saw him in the hospital. Zane throws his arms around her while Chloe chokes with laughter and tears.

"What the hell are you looking at?" Zane tilts his head to glare at the guards at the door. "Untie her before I cut your heads off."

The guards hurry to free Chloe of the ropes, and I notice blazing red marks on her skin where the ropes have been pressing, a clear sign she'd been in them for most of the time she'd been here, if not all, and once again my hatred for Michael is enflamed to its original magnitude.

"What's she doing here?" Chloe shoots me an irritated look, encircling her wrist with her fingers, and I realize I've never been on good terms with her.

Although my feelings for her have softened over the week while she was kidnapped, she has no idea about the sacrifices I was ready to make to rescue her, and must still be thinking of me as a superficial gold-digger ready to do anything immoral to make money, including filling the position of a wealthy businessman's fake girlfriend.

"She was trying to help." Zane defends me as he helps her up, but the doubtful look on Chloe's face is proof she's not easy to convince when it comes to whom to trust.

"Where's Diana?" I ask, scanning around the room. Zane glares at the guards for an answer, and one of them holds his hand out toward the door and replies with fear in his voice, "She's in the room next door."

"Get her here now!" Zane orders and then turns to Chloe. "Did they hurt you? Tell me now, so I can fucking smash their bully heads in."

"They didn't do anything Father didn't order." Chloe wobbles as she walks toward the door after the guards. "How did you find me?" Her eyes skim me up and down as she walks past me.

Zane gives her a quick summary about the boycott and Michael's health as we all follow Chloe out. I come to a sudden stop in the hall when I see the girl the two bodyguards are holding, more carrying than holding because the girl is about to collapse on the floor.

As opposed to Chloe's surprising wellbeing, this girl is nothing but bruises, blood, and ripped clothes. My stomach revolts and I run forward and punch the men to free the girl from their hold.

"Oh, my God, what did they do to her?" I scream in shock as I try to wrap the girl's arm around my shoulder so I can keep her up.

"Diana," Chloe shrieks and hurries to hold the other arm of the girl, and we both help her walk downstairs on her wobbly legs. "It's my fault. I'm so sorry, Diana."

Diana is too beaten-up and pained to reply. Her lips are swollen with a cut on the side, her eyes sunken, her cheeks stained with dried blood. I can't even begin to imagine what they did to her, but the condition of her clothes tells me multiple rapes were a part of her daily routine.

I hear Zane yelling threats after threats as we lay Diana on the backseat of my car. As soon as I get behind the wheel and turn the engine on, I smash my hand on the horn to call Zane.

I'm so angry, I could burn down the entire mansion and the criminals residing in it, at the same time worried that they might strike back and get Zane down. While waiting for Zane, I dial 9-1-1 to report the crime and give the address for the police to corner those filthy men before they can escape. I lock the doors and keep my hands on the wheel, ready to drive away if the guards decide to attack us.

Police cruisers arrive as Zane appears at the door. The guards pathetically try to get into their trucks in an attempt to escape, but the officers stop them before they can get a chance to insert their keys into the ignition. Zane remains with the officers while I drive Chloe and Diana to the nearest hospital.

My nerves are about to explode as I try to kill time in yet another waiting room of a hospital while waiting for a nurse or a doctor to inform me about Chloe and Diana's conditions. Contrary to Michael, neither of the girls deserves to be here, and to think their pain is caused by Michael makes me want to drive back to the hospital he's in and get back the life I gifted him.

How he could hurt so many people is beyond me, not to forget his pathetic apology on his deathbed. I seriously hope hell exists so he'll at least get some punishment for what he did to so many people, because some malignant lung tumor doesn't really cover the bill he has to pay.

I jump to my feet when Chloe appears in the hallway, wiping tears away from her cheeks, and run toward her.

"They're going to operate on her," Chloe says. "A doctor said her ribcage was severely injured and she has internal bleeding." She covers her face with both hands and starts crying. "All she did was to provide me a place to stay. That's what she got in exchange for trying to help me."

"I'm so sorry." My hands instinctively find her shoulders, and I pull her in for a hug. She wraps her arms around me and rests her face on my shoulder, sobbing and shedding more tears. "Where is he?" she asks.

"In Cedars-Sinai."

"Can you drive me there?"

"Sure."

She straightens up, letting go of my hold, and leaves her phone number by the check-in so they can call her if Diana's condition changes. She doesn't speak, but doesn't cry either, as we drive back to Cedars-Sinai. Letting out a long breath, she straightens her black shirt and blue jeans as she knocks on the door of Michael's room. After some hesitation, I decide to go in with her to ensure her safety.

Matilda welcomes her with an introduction and an attempt to hug, but Chloe takes a step back to avoid any physical contact with her and heads straight to Michael's bed. Michael is sleeping with an oxygen mask covering his mouth and nose and doesn't wake up until Chloe calls him by his name.

"Wake up, Michael," Chloe says with a soft melody attached to her words, her face twisted and scary. "You have to hear an important tidbit before death acquires you." A creepy smile curls her lips up, making the hair on my neck stand up.

Michael's eyes slowly open and grow wide when the

realization of who is standing before him hits him. "Chloe, my baby girl," he whispers through the oxygen mask.

"Yeah, right. I'm your baby girl. The baby girl you tried to protect against evil and destructive men for years. The baby girl for whom you didn't blink an eye to punish any boy who tried to approach me. You want to know what happened at the end of your efforts? You want to know how your baby girl ended up?" Her smile grows into startling laughter, and I feel like I'm watching a horror movie where Chloe is the murderer and Michael is the innocent.

"Chloe, what's the matter?" Michael urges, his features reflecting all the love and affection he must be feeling for his daughter.

"The matter is, Daddy, I'm not a virgin anymore. After twenty-five years of abstinence, the men you hired to imprison me gang-raped me. Have you heard of that term, Daddy? Huh, gang-raping? In case you haven't, it's all five men who were supposed to guard the mansion taking turns to fuck me. They didn't beat me up, no. They didn't touch me in that way, but they fucked my brains out for an entire night long."

Michael's face freezes, but the shock and dismay are clear on his widened eyes, and raised eyebrows. Matilda yelps an "Oh, my God," and drops down on a chair, covering her mouth. I'm all ears, despite the guilt that I couldn't have done anything to help her.

"Five men, each one fucked me five times, flushed their disgusting fluids inside me, laughed at me when I cried in pain. You left me alone with them, Daddy. You paid them to be close to me, watch over me. You couldn't have arranged it better if you'd planned on having men use me sexually. Are you happy now,

Daddy?"

Michael's body begins trembling while he chokes and struggles for breath. Chloe grips his wrists to keep him in place while lowering her head over his face. I fear she might bite his nose off with the subtle anger twisting her features.

"One more thing you have to hear before you go. I never ever loved you. Never ever thought you deserved to be my father. Now, I'm telling it to your face; you're not my father." She shoves his arms, causing Michael's already quivering body to shake.

The machine connected to Michael's body screams out loud beeps, and a group of doctors and nurses stride into the room, while one of them orders us out. From the doorway, I watch them as they rip open Michael's clothes to press the defibrillator paddles against his chest.

Matilda doesn't have the courage to see her brother fighting against death and sinks into a chair beside the door, hands covering her face, while Chloe is watching the doctors and the nurses without blinking an eye as they battle to save Michael. As soon as the doctor announces the time of Michael's death as 14:07, though, she tears her gaze from the door and turns to me with a wide grin on her face.

Trying not to hold on to the fact that Michael's time of death has seven and its multiple in it, I see from the corner of my eye that Matilda rushes back inside the room, screaming and crying.

"I'm so sorry," I say to Chloe, referring to the raping incident.

The same chilling smile resumes its place on her lips. "Don't be. His number came up a long time ago."

"I meant the rape. It's my fault. Michael kidnapped you to keep me under control. I swear I tried to convince him to let you go."

With her eyebrows pulling together and the corner of her lips curving down, she gives her head a little shake in disbelief. "Why would he think he could control you through me? I'm nobody to you."

"You're not nobody to me. You're Ace's sister, but more importantly you're an innocent person. Michael must have guessed that I couldn't possibly do anything to endanger an innocent person, be it the sister of the man I love or the next girl on the street. But apparently all my efforts were in vain. They hurt you and Diana. I'm so sorry."

Her eyes drop down to the floor, then come back to me, and she looks at me with the same pain I see frequently on Ace's face. They might not be related by blood, but their expressions couldn't have been more similar than that of biological siblings.

"Diana will hopefully recover, but don't worry about me. Nobody raped me. No one would dare touch His Majesty's only daughter. I lied in there. I've wanted to hurt him so badly for all of my life, I had to do it at his weakest time to finally take my lifelong revenge on him."

I let out a laugh, but it's more like a pathetic shriek of shock than anything else. "It didn't look like a lie to me in there," I chime in. "You couldn't possibly be lying to me to make me feel better, could you? I prefer honesty to a fake state of relief."

She shakes her head, smiling, but this time in a friendly and affectionate manner, rather than the scary smiles she gifted to her father in his last seconds. "I'll see you around."

Slipping her hair off of her shoulders, she spins around on her heels and heads straight toward the exit, her posture taller and prouder with each step, carrying zero trace of a girl who's just lost her father.

Michael is now dead, and I don't know how his death could be related to seven since seven is the root of evil in my eyes. Then a cold shiver courses through my body as the realization hits me that today's date is September the 7th.

CH 6 - The Lie

I rush through the sliding doors and jump into the elevator down to the parking lot. While dealing with Michael and Chloe, I've completely forgotten about Ace and Edward's scheme to take advantage of him. He had his men ready in case Ace didn't willingly give himself to him. As much as I hated Michael, I wish it was Edward who died, rather than Michael.

As I run toward my car, I dial Pleasure Extraordinaire, since I have no hope of getting Ace to answer me if I call his cell. Alexander is the one whom I have to wrestle with again to locate Ace.

"Alexander, hello. Is Ace there? Is he all right?"

"Yes, Miss. He's in his office. However, we're swamped with clients today. I can schedule an appointment for you for tomorrow?"

Had I known Alexander would be this uncooperative, I'd have asked for Laila's or JJ's phone number to ask about Ace. They'd be more helpful than Alexander will ever be. "I don't need an appointment to talk to my boyfriend." There I've said it. Although it sounds foreign, Ace was the one who first claimed me as his. "I have to talk to him about an urgent matter. Can you please tell him I'll be there in half an hour?" Without waiting for a reply, I disconnect and get into my car.

I start the engine and slide out of the parking lot to the main street, imagining how Ace must be interviewing some horny, rich women with his blood-scorching interrogative questions. Contrary to my shyness when I was interviewed, those cock-hungry women will interpret his questions as an invitation or as foreplay and request him to be their playmate.

Although he claims he doesn't service the clients sexually, it's not a rule carved in stone. With his state of mind, he might easily be convinced and end up in yet another woman's bed—that's if he hasn't already had sex with someone else last night.

Argh, this obscurity is killing me. I have to know if he's been faithful to me and I have to inform him about the details of Zane's tricks to get into my pants. And what the hell happened to Edward?

My heart is drumming fast as I hand the car key to the valet; a young man, whose face I don't recognize, takes my arm, and walks me through the front door. Two lines of young and muscled men greet me at the entrance, all unfamiliar. I've spent enough time here to at least recognize some faces, but no.

The unfamiliarity continues in the decoration as the man next to me escorts me down the long hall toward Ace's office. No more flowers beautifying the walls, no heart-warming lighting effects welcoming the guests, just plain and headache-inducing red lights and empty red walls and red carpets.

As we turn the corner to the hall that leads to Ace's hall, my escort respectfully directs me toward a set of armchairs next to a tall window and requests me to wait until Ace is finished with his client. At least he's with a client and not with Edward.

"Have you seen Edward Neuberger come in today?" I ask.

"I'm sorry but I can't give away confidential

information about our clients," he replies with an apologetic look on his face.

"He's not a client here. Pleasure Extraordinaire serves women, not men," I add, though I understand his obligation to remain silent about everything he sees. "Whatever." I shrug and throw myself in the armchair that's facing Ace's office door.

The interview or whatever Ace is doing with his client in there continues even after half an hour. A bare-chested, blond man brings a glass of club soda and crackers for me, and I eat them like a starving woman, while watching Ace's office door like a blockbuster movie.

After forty minutes and still no sign of Ace, I drop the glass, gather my purse, and stride toward his office. I knock on the door and wait to give Ace and his client time to get their acts together if they're practicing any sexual activity, although that possibility revolts my stomach.

What if it is actually the reality? What if I find Ace sucking another woman's pussy on his desk, just like he did to me a few days ago, or squirming while having his cock sucked? It'll crush my heart, but then again Zane did both with me just a few hours ago.

Holding my breath, I open the door and glance directly at Ace, who's standing in front of a young, tall, blonde woman. Judging by her giggles, I've caught them in the middle of an amusing conversation.

A pang of jealousy rushes through me at the intimacy of their postures, so close to each other, although there's no tangible sign of sexual intercourse.

Ace is wearing a light-blue shirt, the top buttons undone, sleeves folded up to the elbows, revealing the delicious skin and muscles underneath. His blond hair is tied into a loose ponytail, several strands falling over his cheeks and neck.

The sight of him, so handsome and arousing, makes my heart skip a beat. I feel like I'm falling in love with him all over again. My body begs me to run and throw myself at him, unite with his gorgeous body, press my breasts against him, and wrap my legs around his hips.

But, his one-second glance at me shows he doesn't reciprocate any of the emotions I feel for him. He only mutters a dry "Hello," and then turns his attention back to the blonde.

The indifference and lack of interest on his face, in his voice, as if I'm one of his employees and not the girl he's supposed to have feelings for, breaks my heart as much as it would have if I'd caught him licking the blonde's cunt.

"May I come in?" I ask, hesitant and feeling strange in his presence, uncomfortable with the physical and emotional distance separating us.

"Tina, would you give me a minute? I'll see you afterwards," Ace tells the blonde, totally ignoring my question. The blonde reaches up and squeezes Ace's forearm before heading toward the door. My heart breaks in two as I see Ace wink at her while she leaves.

Ace invites me in with a nod, inhaling a long breath, and settles in his chair, and offers me the chair before his desk with a gesture of his hand.

No hug or friendly hello.

I'd rather have him pouring out his anger at me for last night than facing the cold, uninterested Ace, who might or might not go to the blonde afterwards to have sex with her.

Tentatively, I take my place on the chair and place my purse on my lap. I'm burning with the desire to ask him who the girl is, but it's not the right moment to reveal my jealous side to him just yet. "About last night," I start but he cuts me off with his hand. "Please, let me explain."

"You don't need to."

"I won't go anywhere until you hear everything in detail."

He rolls his eyes, and they drift away from me and land on the screen of his computer.

"I was in the bedroom next door while Edward talked to you last night. I overheard everything he said. And more than that, he asked his men to be prepared to take you down if you didn't obey. I wanted to spare you the trauma."

I see his Adam's apple move up and down as he swallows, but besides that, he's still and gazing at his computer.

"I didn't know what to do, so I called Zane."

Hearing Zane's name makes the corner of his lip twitch.

"He told me he could help you," I continue. "He told me about his plans to end Michael's position in HMG and promised to stop Edward from hurting you. But he wanted me in exchange for his help. I... I didn't know what else to do. I panicked. I couldn't see any other option to help you."

He makes an 'hmm' sound and nods, still keeping his eyes locked on the computer screen.

"I don't like him at all. In fact I hate him. You're the only man I care about, Ace. You're the only man I love." A love confession? I should have seen it coming.

According to my aunt, a girl should never be the first one to reveal her feelings and let the man take the initiative. I see now the merit in her words, because Ace doesn't respond like the lover whose heart hosts the same turmoil of feelings.

"Please, say something. Tell me that you'll forgive me. I did it for you," I beg, ready to go down to my knees and cry until I get a response out of him.

Despite a sob that makes my voice tremble, I keep on reciting the events. "You must have heard it from the news. Michael had a heart attack and died. We found Chloe and Diana. Chloe is fine, well, at least physically, but Diana is in a bad condition and has to have a surgery today."

Ace spins his head to me so fast I fear his neck will break. "Where? Which hospital?" he asks with worry coating his voice and dominating his expression. My chest constricts in pain at his response to the news, but not to me. He rises, grabbing his navy-blue leather jacket, and slides into it.

"Ace, please. There's nothing you can do about Diana at this point. They won't let you see her until after the surgery. Can we first talk about our problem?"

He takes a step toward me, a faint smile appearing on his lips. "I have an apology to make. I don't know how to say it, so I'll just say it as it comes. I don't have any feelings for you. At least not the type of feelings you expect me to have."

He rubs his forehead and runs his fingers through his hair. "There's no better way to say it, but I just used you. First it was to annoy Zane because I was aware of his interest in you, then to rescue my sister. You seemed to be willing to help me find her, and I could get insider information about Michael through you. And, let's face it," he pauses with a brief laugh, "you were even ready to have sex with Michael's friends to help me out. I mean, how could I say no to such an enormous favor? I just kept feeding your feelings about me, but sorry I just don't feel any deep emotions for you. You'll call me a jerk and I completely agree with you. But hey, I'm here whenever you want to hook up. You're hot and I'm definitely not the kind of man to turn down a horny chick."

"What are you talking about?" I jump to my feet, despite the state of complete shock that has my body paralyzed, and stride toward him, my hands up and ready to take him down. "Are you fucking kidding me? Was everything a lie? It can't be. You're just ..."

My tongue loses its ability to roll out the words as my mind begins to grasp more and more of his revelation. The vein in my forehead pulses as warmth reaches up my cheeks. Breath leaves my lungs in short and quick intervals while I fight hard against the tremor that's overtaking my body.

"I know it's shit and I'm really sorry about that. But yeah, I'm not the man you thought I was. What else can I say? You shouldn't have expected a serious commitment from a man who runs a brothel, right? I mean, come on. It just defies logic in every sense. You're supposed to be a smart girl with a double major and everything."

I feel bile rising up in my throat. I swallow it down and fist my hands to stop them from trembling. "Are you fucking saying it was my fault that I fell for your lies? You're not just a jerk. You're a filthy pig like your brother and your father. But you're not as good a lover in bed as your brother is. Zane fucked me hard and forced two intense orgasms out of me you wouldn't have pulled out in weeks to come."

"Now that's just mean. Tell me which hospital Diana is staying at and get the fuck off my property."

"Go figure it out by yourself. I'm done with trying to save your sorry ass." With that I spin around and rush out of his office.

I don't remember any details of how I end up in my

car but when my senses come back to me, I find myself crying against the steering wheel of my car in the parking lot of a diner I've never seen or heard of before. I'm still going through the biggest blow of my life.

Among all the people I thought could hurt me, Ace was the one who impaled the deadly arrow into my heart, and I feel the pain he's caused will be a steady accompaniment until I find a way to erase him from my mind and from my heart.

The Hawkins men, each and every one of them, managed to harm me one way or another, and I wonder what the merit of my involvement in their lives was or theirs into mine.

Shouldn't everything be happening for a reason?

It seems like the only thing to came out of my encounter with them was to get my heart slashed into a thousand pieces. Am I supposed to be coming out of this stronger or fearless? Is that it? Life's way to bolster me up?

I wish I had my mom with me; at least I'd have someone to lean on, a shoulder to cry out my pain on. Taylor is neck-deep with her own worries as is; I can't add yet another drop into her full glass.

I open the door to get out of my car and look up to the dark sky. It's chilly and the hair on my arms rises in response to the wind.

"Mom, if you're out there somewhere, if you can hear me, please help me get out of this."

Tears well up in my eyes, blocking my sight, but I continue staring at the stars lighting up the darkness. Will I be able to bring the light back into my heart? Seems impossible because I already miss Ace, yearn for the feeling of warmth and safety I had in his arms. But not the Ace I met today, not the one who used me, but the one he pretended to be.

It's silly how I could fall for an imaginary persona, a fantasy like a Disney prince. My mind is ready to get over him, but it'll take long days filled with tears and sobs to convince my heart to move on.

"Mom," I call out again. "Help me forget him."

CH 7 - The Life After - ACE

Pain. And anger. Those are the constant occupants in my heart since the day Lindsay stormed out of my office without any sign of coming back. Work isn't sufficient to hold my attention for more than half an hour before my mind twirls back to her. I've never been into alcohol and I won't start looking to it as a means to erase her out of my mind.

Other women?

Let's just say I'm cock-blocked and the thought of coming close to any woman who's not Lindsay irks me in ways that the idea of becoming a monk doesn't sound ridiculous. Sleep is the only time I can forget she's gone from my life, and if I'm lucky, she shows her beautiful face to me in my dreams.

Just like now.

She's in my arms, her breasts pushing against my ribcage, her hand splayed open on my chest right above my heart. Her head resting on my shoulder, she's staring into my eyes and whispers her love to me.

Her cheeks flush with a shy smile as she's waiting to hear how I'm about to respond. My heart speeds up with the knowledge that my feeling for her is mutual, and that she won't let me down and will respect what we have.

I open my mouth, move my lips, ready to lay out the wild emotions she's causing in my heart, but my tongue doesn't roll. It objects to speaking out the truth and remains frozen inside my mouth. Her eyes grow with anticipation, her eyebrows up close to her hairline.

I straighten up and try one more time ... in vain. My tongue fails me; my voice is gone.

She moves away from me, her expression lacking the sweetness that I've grown addicted to. Her eyes size me up and down with disdain, her lips pursed tightly.

I know what she's about to say. I know what's coming. She opens her lovely mouth, her eyes now glaring at me.

"I thought you were man enough to own your emotions," she spits out the words one by one. She pulls her body away from me, and a sudden coldness settles inside me. "Fine. Fortunately, you're not irreplaceable. Zane is much better than you in so many ways."

I struggle to move forward and grab her hand before she totally abandons me. But she runs away before I can catch her and tell her the only truth my heart beats for. I stride toward the direction she's escaped and hear faint sounds of sobs from far away. I know those sounds. I've heard them for the majority of my life.

Forgetting all about Lindsay, I change my way toward the sounds and come to a sudden halt in front of a door. It's Irene. She's hiding in her bedroom again to cry.

My heart stops, and I wonder what among the dozens of reasons caused her sorrow this time, her unrequited love for Michael, the countless restrictions in her life, Michael's horrid abuses to Chloe? The list is long.

I open the door with a kick and rush through the darkness to find my mother. Her cries break my heart, and I run faster to sooth her pain and calm her down. I find her lying on her bed, hiding beneath the covers. Gently, I pull them away and whisper to her the same lie everyone who knows Michael's abusive personality has been repeating to her over and over.

"Everything is gonna be all right."

I reach up and touch her hand, but instead of its usual warmth, it's cold and covered with thick liquid.

Panicked, I look for the light switch and turn on the light on the night stand. The sight of dark-red blood blinds my eyes, but I hurry to find the cut to stop more blood from gushing out.

"Mother, no. Don't do that to me. Don't leave me," I cry, shaking her lifeless arms. "Don't go. Stay with me. I can't live without you. Mother, open your eyes!"

Her body is heavy. Thick strands of hair are plastered on her face. Blood is spilling out of her wrists like an uninhibited river. I know she's gone for good, no matter how hard I try to bring her back.

I push away the hair to see her face one last time and to tell her how much I love her. But I freeze and drop down on my knees as I realize it's not Irene, but Lindsay lying dead on the bed.

I jerk and jump up in bed, snapping my eyes open, and let out a loud breath of relief as I realize I'm in my bedroom in Pleasure Extraordinaire, and it was but a horrible nightmare. However, that fact doesn't stop a violent shiver from coursing through my body.

Today marks the thirteenth day since I ordered Lindsay out of my office and not a minute has passed when I haven't wished I could take back the words I said to her.

I roll over on the bed and grab the pillow she used to sleep on to inhale it, but it doesn't smell like her anymore, neither do the clothes she left in my apartment. Those are the only things from her that are left to me, the only proof of the short-lived happiness I experienced for the first time with a woman, other than my mother and Chloe.

I hold the pillow in my arms tightly anyway and inhale it one last time to catch her scent, trying not to think if she's waking up in Zane's arms right now.

I glance at my phone to see it's already seven fifteen. Thank goodness I have work to distract me. After a quick shower, I settle before my desk to go over the details related to a new client, whom I'll be interviewing in half an hour. However, it's not an easy task since my mind keeps wandering back to the nightmare.

I pull open the drawer to retrieve a pair of Lindsay's black panties that I keep for occasions like this to calm my nerves. She must be fine, I think to myself. More than fine, actually. Zane must be providing her with whatever she needs until he meets his next victim.

I shake my head to focus back on the file before me. A new client, but unlike my other clients, she's tested positive for STDs. I've never turned down a client, and I won't change my habit now either. Especially for someone like her who was direct and honest about her test results from early on.

Although I've talked with her on the phone a few times, today will be the first time I'll meet her in person.

Even with the rarity of her situation, which should keep my attention focused, the words on the screen fly away and are replaced with Lindsay's face. I'm so done with it, I'm only minutes away from throwing everything away for a vacation to forget the painful past.

I've lived for my work. It's my life's accomplishment. Lindsay had to take away the only thing I felt proud to have. Even Michael couldn't come that close to wiping my motivation from me.

The icon of the security camera pops out on the computer screen, and I click on it to see the new client entering through the front gate and drop Lindsay's panties back into the drawer. She looks younger than the age she stated in her application, but every bit as wealthy with her designer clothes, perfectly fitting the profile of my clientele.

In a few minutes, I welcome her into my office. She's medium height with thick black hair and olive skin, hinting at her Hispanic or Italian heritage, and wearing a beige summer dress with flared skirt.

She shakes my hand with a strange mixture of confidence and shyness and takes a chair in front of my desk. I phone Alexander to tell him not to put through any calls for the morning, and then turn to my client.

"Mrs. Attisano, I'm honored to have you as a client at Pleasure Extraordinaire and would like to assure you that everything that happens inside my establishment will remain secret no matter what. We go to great lengths to ensure utmost confidentiality and continue seeking ways to identify and eliminate any potential dangers along the way."

"That's calming," Simone Attisano replies. "Please, call me Simone."

"All right, Simone. As we discussed on the phone, we've never had a client with an STD before, but let me thank you once again for not letting that information deter you from considering our services."

She takes a long breath and drops her eyes to the wedding ring that she's been playing with since she sat on the chair. "I guess I owe you an explanation."

"You don't need to explain anything to me. You're welcome to use our services as much as our other clients."

"Please, I'll feel more comfortable if I can get it out of my heart."

With my nod, she begins her story. "I've only been

with one man in my life. My husband. I gave him four beautiful children and my youth, and he gave me herpes. Now I'm thirty-four and facing a life-long loneliness thanks to his special gift. I can't divorce him, both because of our kids and our business. That, however, doesn't mean that he won't be punished for what he did to me. He agreed to transfer to me half of his assets without question. I'm not the type of woman who'd pursue a man for sex. I'd rather pay for the satisfaction I need than chase some jerks who might or might not call afterwards. Besides, I don't want to spread the disease to innocent people either. That's why I've been in search of a service like yours, and when I heard about you through a friend, who's also a member here, I had to give it a try. Oh, and by the way, my husband will pay for the expenses I'll have here, so don't shy away from offering me your most expensive suites and services." She gives me a brief smile, revealing the satisfaction she's getting at the punishment she's chosen for her husband.

Exactly the kind of client I'm happy to have. "I can't say it's been easy to find a lover for you who is also infected with herpes as well as who carries the qualifications you requested, but no challenge is too big for us when it comes to customer satisfaction, and I'm happy to say we found a man suitable for your needs and wishes."

"That fast?"

I retrieve a tablet from the top drawer and hand it to her. "Here're some pictures and a video of him. His name is Sergio and he's twenty-nine. If you find him attractive, I'll schedule for you to meet him right after our talk. He's in the last stage of his training, which should be complete by the end of the upcoming week. But, you're welcome to go ahead and test him, if you so wish. You can either talk to him about the areas he needs improvement or inform me so I can make sure he's well-equipped for all your wishes."

"Let me see." The instant she glances at the screen of the tablet, her eyes grow large and her jaw drops open. Exactly the reaction I strive for from my clients. "Wow, is he for real? Lord. He's good. How tall is he?"

"Six foot one."

"Like my husband, but this one is way, way hotter than him," she adds with a giggle. Even mature women can't keep themselves from acting like a teenager in the presence of a good-looking man, literally or digitally. "I wish my husband could see this." She throws out loud laughter, and I realize she's not here to satisfy her own sexual needs but to get revenge on her husband. Whatever her reasons might be though, I can't turn her down.

"Does that mean you want to meet him?"

"Hell, yeah. Nothing can stop me."

"All right, then. Let me send Sergio a memo to inform him of your visit." I type a quick message to Sergio, the latest addition to my permanent crew, and turn my attention back to Simone. "Sergio is willing to offer you a special discount where you can hire him for a full month for fifteen thousand dollars, and he'll be all yours, which means he won't be attending to any other clients while he's committed to you and you can spend as much time with him as you want."

"Today must be my lucky day. I'll take his offer, but under one condition."

"Which is..."

"Instead of fifteen, make it twenty as a courtesy to my husband." She laughs again and rubs her palms together, looking giddy with excitement.

"The first meeting is on the house," I remind her as I do for all the new members. "After the meeting, please come back to sign the agreement so we can make your membership official." I call Nick to escort Simone out to Sergio's suite and shake hands with her before she leaves my office.

I rented the Summer Suite to Sergio, although now I'm thinking I should have just closed down that filthy room where Zane fucked Lindsay, and filled it with bricks like they do to the thirteenth floors for the number's infamous unluckiness.

With fury surfacing back inside me, I head back to my desk. The phone rings just when I sit back in my chair, its incessant tune jolting my already damaged nerves, and I grab the receiver with all the anger fuming inside me, and yell, "Didn't I say no interruptions for the morning?" Alex is on the receiving end of my outrage and apologizes. "Someone named Mrs. Garnett wants to see you urgently."

"Tell her that I'm in a meeting. Come on. Produce a lie." I start to place the receiver back when the realization suddenly strikes me. "Wait, Alexander. Did you say Garnett? Is her name Taylor?" I ask, although I fail to see what Lindsay's sister can be doing here, unless... The fresh details of my nightmare rush through my mind. Oh, God, is Lindsay all right? "Send her in. Hurry," I say and hang up.

I stand in front of the windows and nervously run my other hand through my hair, trying to tone down my worry about Lindsay and the numerous things that might have happened to her. She's not the type of girl to attempt suicide, but that doesn't take away the possibility of her being hurt by an infinite number of causalities; traffic accident, sickness, attack.

Perhaps that's why she hasn't initiated any contact with me.

That realization is disturbing, as well as comforting, since it might mean she's not over me yet and was only prevented by circumstances outside of her control.

CH 8 - The Mind Fuck - ACE

The door swings open with a loud thud, and I turn to see Lindsay's older sister, Taylor, sporting one of the angriest faces I've seen in my life. She looks like dynamite ready to explode. What's with Doheny girls and their anger issues? She can easily compete with Michael in terms of spreading fear with just a glare.

"You," she spits the word out and lifts her hand to point her index finger at me. "You're going to pay for what you did to my sister."

Shit. It's happening. My nightmare must be coming true, and it's me who has caused Lindsay to do whatever she did. "Mrs. Garnett. Taylor." I lift my hands up in the air as a gesture to calm her down. "Please tell me what's going on. The last thing I want is for Lindsay to be hurt. We separated two weeks ago, and that was the last time I've heard from her."

"I don't have the faintest fucking idea what's going on with her," Taylor yells. "She stopped talking to me. She's not letting me into her apartment. She stopped eating altogether. What did you do to my sister that she turned against me so much so that she won't talk to me anymore?"

My hands drop to either side of my body, and I lower my head with pain as I remember the last day I saw her. "She slept with Zane, and after that we broke up."

"That's a lie. My sister doesn't go behind someone she

95

loves." Shock and skepticism replace her anger, and she throws herself to the chair beside her.

"It's not a lie. I saw them with my own eyes. She had her reasons, but it doesn't change the facts." My chest tightens again as it always does when I think about that night when Lindsay chose Zane over me.

"I had no idea. But, she's clearly suffering. I've never seen her like that. She's in a great deal of pain. You have to help me. Please go and see her, at least, and talk things out."

"I don't think it's a good idea, besides I can't do it. I'm not emotionally in a good place myself, either."

She rolls her eyes then narrows them at me. "Clearly, you're strong enough to see clients. Haven't you heard any of what I said?" Her voice rises, scratching my ears. "She's not eating and she probably won't until she talks to you. You and your family put her through so much you owe it to her to at least talk to her."

She's right, of course. Lindsay came close to risking her life to save Chloe, but it doesn't change the fact that she ran to Zane at the first sign of trouble rather than coming to me.

"Please, don't let my sister down. She must be really regretting her mistake. Here's the key to her apartment. Go see her for yourself. But be warned, she gets very aggressive toward visitors." She opens her purse to fish out a key, stands up, moving toward me, and grabs my hand to place the key in my palm. "If you have or had any feelings for her, you wouldn't let her suffer. Please, go talk to her before it's too late."

I squeeze my hand, pushing the key into my flesh as I watch Taylor exit my office. As much as I'm dying to see Lindsay again, just the thought of having to relive the minutes Zane had Lindsay is painful enough to knock me out.

I stroll into my office, then out in the hall while trying to decide what to do. Although Taylor might see a potential benefit in my visit, it won't do any good to Lindsay, because I'm not ready to forget the past.

I won't lie and say I'm ready to take her back just to sooth her momentarily. Although a part of me wants nothing but that, it's not gonna happen. Not only will she hate me more for lying to her, but also she'll hurt more when she finds out the truth in the future.

The logical thing to do is to let her take her time to get over the pain on her own terms. But if she really refuses to eat, like Taylor said, that can end really badly. What helps me decide seeing her one last time is actually a good idea is the fact that I was an asshole to her in our last meeting. Now that my head is clearer than it was two weeks ago, I might manage to explain my disappointment to her, without further hurting her feelings.

I slide the key to her apartment into my pocket and head out. My hands tremble as I wrap my fingers around the steering wheel, and once again I'm reminded that Lindsay has been the only woman who could make me nervous. Why couldn't she simply choose me as her equal partner in everything, in bed and in trouble? Why did she have to allow Zane to use her that way?

I hurry to the neighborhood she lives in but take my time to find a parking spot and also to garner more confidence to face her. What am I going to do if she cries and begs for me to take her back? I won't have any power left to decline her, especially because I miss her, too. Very much.

But what she did to me will remain engraved in my mind permanently. I can't help feeling like a pussy. Perhaps that's why she chose Zane rather than coming first to me. She had to fucking protect me. Who is she thinking I am? A fucking child?

I take the stairs since the elevator looks suspiciously unsteady, and I have no will to deal with being stuck in a malfunctioning elevator. My heart pushes harder and harder against my chest as I climb the blue-carpeted stairs.

I stop in front of her door. It's too much to take in, being separated by a wall only, after not having seen her for two long weeks. With each second, I become more convinced that it'll be me who will beg for her to take me back. I can't believe she provokes so much inside me that I can't breathe without her.

I knock on the door despite the key in my palm. When she doesn't respond, I unlock the door, step in, and am immediately hit by a warm wave of disgusting odor.

"What the hell," I curse, covering my mouth and nose with both hands as the only way to protect myself from throwing up, and close the door with a kick. Pieces of clothing are tossed on the floor and sofa in the living room, along with pizza boxes and unopened soda cans. Litter and trash as far as the eye can see.

I push open a pizza box and see its contents untouched. Taylor might be telling the truth about Lindsay not eating anything.

I walk through the living room to open the windows and gather a plastic bag to get rid of the uneaten food, while keeping my ears on alert mode for any sound that may come from Lindsay's bedroom.

Even after I tie up the plastic bag, the intense smell is still there. I follow my nose and enter the kitchen to go through her fridge. Uncooked chicken, a couple of half-eaten cans of chili, French cheese, and decayed lettuce. The fridge will need some thorough disinfecting in order to use it again.

Putting the entire contents of the fridge into another plastic bag, I carry both bags down to the dumpster.

The second time I enter her apartment, she welcomes me with a snarl from her bedroom. "Taylor, I said I'm not hungry. I'll call the police if you don't leave now."

"I'm not Taylor," I yell back and push open her bedroom door. If I thought her fridge was reeking, I have no words for the smell inside the bedroom; it's powerful enough to put me out. "Fuck! What's that smell? Have you taken a skunk as your roommate? It smells fucking horrible in here."

She jolts up from her bed and pulls the covers over her wrinkled clothes, while staring at me with shock and embarrassment.

"Wait a minute." My eyes grow wide as I realize the source of the deadly smell. "Weren't you wearing that blouse and skirt the last time you came to my office? That was almost two weeks ago? Haven't you showered and changed clothes since then?"

"Fuck you. Why do you care?" She gets up to her feet and throws the bed covers down, not ashamed anymore of her clothes or smell. "Get the fuck out of my apartment before I call the police. I don't want to see your fucking face again."

She's using my words against me, which goes to show she must be thinking about them over and over again, just like the minutes she spent in Zane's arms keep coming back at me.

"Look, Lindsay. No man is worth this." I point at her clothes with two hands. "Especially a man like me, who needs saving." I'm not sure why I've said that, but it seems I can't forget about my own injured ego even for a minute.

She reaches down and grabs her cellular. "Go now, or I'll call 9-1-1."

"Yes, please. Go ahead and do that. They should send a fire truck to flush the dirt off your body."

"Hahaha, very funny." She lifts her phone and dials. First I think she's mocking me, but then when I hear through on the loudspeaker that it's indeed 911 she's dialed, I launch forward to grab her phone.

"There's an intruder in my apartment," she screams as she fights back, but eventually gives in and hands me the phone.

I explain to the lady on the other side that it was a wrong number and hang up. I wrap my arms around her to force her toward the bathroom, but she bites my arm to free herself from my hold, making me yell in pain.

"You smell like a skunk and attack like a wildcat. It's time we put an end to this." I scoop her up despite her struggles to break free and haul her into the bathtub. She punches my face and shoulders as I lean forward to run the water.

The cold water sprinkling down on her makes her scream with shock, and she jumps up to escape it. The sleeves of my shirt are getting wet while I try to keep her in place in the bathtub but she's hard to control. I quickly take off all my clothes except for my boxer briefs and get inside the bathtub beside her.

She's completely soaked but won't stop her attempts to get out. "Let me go. I don't need your help. I can wash myself."

The water turns warmer with time, and I grab a bottle of body wash and squeeze almost all of it down over her head. "Yeah, right. That's why you smell like a dumpster."

She punches my chest as I shampoo her hair,

intentionally smearing her eyes with it so she won't see where she's throwing her fists.

Taking advantage of her momentary blindness, I rip off her blouse and skirt so I can wash her body too. Her arms instantly cover her chest, and I chuckle at her attempt to hide the body I saw completely naked and fucked many times.

On second thought, she's right at doing so, because my cock twitches at the sight of the outlines of her breasts beneath her bra, of the water and foam dripping from her flawless stomach down to her ... Fuck.

She still smells like a taco fart, but it won't stop me from getting hard for her. She has the reins to my cock. That's all there is to it.

"My eyes are burning," she screams and reaches for her face, and I hurry to unclip her bra and forcefully pull it off her arms.

When I move down to tug away her panties, my lips touch her shoulder, and that brief touch makes her stop fighting against me. If I knew kissing her would calm her down, I'd have tried it earlier. But she won't spread her legs wide enough for me to get those fucking panties off her completely.

Ignoring her unwillingness to comply, I begin spreading the foam of the body wash around her shoulders and arms, pushing them aside to rub her breasts clean.

Okay, I admit I work a little longer on her breasts than I did on her shoulders, and my hands clearly shake in the process, but she's not striking back for my inappropriate behavior. No punches or kicks. No curses or threats.

I knead those breasts that plague my dreams every night and pinch at her nipples, while watching her foamed-covered face with amusement. My cock thickens to its full size with the thrill of having fought with her and now having her completely naked, still, and surrendered before me. I consider mouthing her nipples and touching her between her legs.

The water is dripping down her chest, making it impossible for me to think straight. My breathing is heavy as opposed to her unmoving chest. She'd given up on food and hygiene. Doesn't she need air either?

I drop my head on her shoulder and leave a kiss on her skin before kneeling down in front of her and start running my lips down her chest until I get to her nipples. Still unable to move, she draws a sharp breath and gulps when my teeth graze her nipple.

This is completely crazy. I came here to talk about our break up, convince her it's the best for both of us, but my hand is inching down between her legs, and all I can think about is how tight and wet she was the last time I fucked her pussy.

Her body trembles as my fingers settle on her mound and then part the lips of her pussy, sliding in between. Her warm, swollen flesh is a magnet for my hand and I wouldn't be able to stop myself even if I had a clear head, which I don't right now. She squeezes her legs around my hand as my fingers glide over her clit down toward her opening, smearing the foam all around.

"Stop it." Finally she starts breathing and it's coming out short and frantic. She places her hands on my shoulders, possibly to push me away but it feels more like she's trying to keep me in place. "I don't want it. You should go now."

I suck her breast, filling my mouth with it, and slide my finger inside her pussy while pressuring her clit with my thumb.

"Ace, please no. Fuck...let...me...go," she stutters and

shakes. I ignore her fake begging and fill her with my fingers to the hilt, enjoying the feeling of the moist tightness of her insides wrapping around my fingers. It has been too long since I fucked her, and the urge to feel her pussy convulsing around my cock again is too big to resist.

I let her breast free and slowly wander down to where my fingers are, licking her wet skin along the way. Knowing what's about to come, she mutters, "No, no, no, no," but I take her half-hearted request as approval and reach down and swirl my tongue around her clit, while my speeding fingers are fucking her juicy pussy. She spreads her knees and bucks up her hips to my face to give me more skin to enjoy.

I glance up at her in surprise and see her hands cupping her breasts, kneading them ferociously, while she's biting her lower lip, her eyes half-closed. Water is dripping down her face. Her wet hair is messed up and plastered on her forehead and red cheeks.

Many wouldn't give a crap about her looks right now, but I could keep staring at her and admiring her beauty forever. She's perfect. Smooth skin, sensual lips that deserve to be parted with cock on a daily basis, firm breasts, an even firmer ass. So fucking perfect.

She must have noticed my gaze, because she looks down at me, and I notice anger turning her glazed expression into that of a murderer in an instant.

Before I can realize it, she lifts her hand and lands it on my cheek with a slap, startling me, and pulls my hair up so strongly, it hurts. "I said, stop it. I'm with Zane, now. Only he can fuck me," she roars and slaps me again, fixing her crazy eyes on me.

Hearing Zane's name coming out of her lips pushes all the anger I've been trying to forget up to the surface, and for a moment, I lose it. My mind, my sense, my reasoning; all evaporate into thin air with her words.

Getting on my feet, I lift her and push her against the tiles, launching my torso against her to keep her from escaping. She glances at me with fear. I continue and wrap her legs around my hip, while adjusting my rock-hard cock out of my boxer briefs and against her opening.

Her protests come a little too late, just when I cup her ass and slide the head of my cock into her, and even so they sound more like squirms of pleasure than orders for me to stop.

"Ace, no. Oh God." She sighs—no trace of anger apparent in her voice, only confusion and pleasure— and digs her fingernails into my biceps as I drive into her balls-deep.

My head falls against the wet wall, and I pause to take in the mind-fucking ecstasy of feeling her pussy swallowing up my cock hungrily. Whatever she may claim about her disgust for me, she's fucking slick for me all the way inside. And I'd be a liar if I said filling her up and penetrating her the hard way isn't heaven on earth.

"No, no, no. Arghhh. We should stop it. No." She drops her head on my shoulder when I start driving in and out of her. She keeps mumbling no's as if she means 'yes, give it to me, baby, fuck me hard.'

Her body molds easily against mine, soft and fragile, all soaked and hot with water. But rather than the urge to be careful with her, her mind-fucking vulnerability makes me want to manhandle her and force her to her boundaries, to fuck her until she fully surrenders to me.

Her pussy is leaking thin, slippery juice as my cock penetrates it with rough strokes. I know her well enough to guess she'll not want me to know about her climax, won't want to show she's enjoying my cock with all the hatred brewing inside her, but if the violent scratches of her nails on my back and the deep bite of her teeth on my shoulder are a sign of anything, it's that she'll come hard and all over me, and there's nothing she can do to hide it from me.

My beautiful panther can't stop herself from getting off on my cock, but has the nerve to give me physical pain along the way. The pain she's intending to give me however is only making my balls ache with the urge to explode into her as they slap against her flesh.

A loud cry fills her mouth and she stills in my arms, doesn't even breathe, and I know her pussy has reached the satisfaction it has been longing for since... fuck, I shouldn't go there.

"That's my girl," I whisper.

"Ace," she cries while I plunge my release deep inside of her and continue thrusting until her greedy pussy swallows up my last drop. Even though I'm dried to the bone, I'm unwilling to leave her body and face the harsh reality. I want to freeze time and stay in that sweet pussy forever. But the truth is slowly rearing its ugly face and the hazy expression on Lindsay's face is getting replaced with cold bitterness.

"I'm not your girl," Lindsay speaks with a smirk appearing on her lips. "You once again showed me Zane is the better lover."

Her words crash into me so strongly, my head whirls with dizziness. I drop her, cold turkey, leaving her body, and take a step back to avoid more assault from her.

Zane will always be with us, doesn't matter how much I try to ignore it or how addicted my cock is to her pussy; he'll always poke his nose into our lives and remind me of the night he fucked her to orgasm. Fate is one merciless bitch and gave me a woman marked up by none other

LIV BENNETT

than my life-long enemy.

The sneer on Lindsay's face hardens, a deep frown wrinkling her forehead. She claims she did it to protect me, but I saw it with my own eyes on the security cameras. She enjoyed his cock, took him deep inside of her, let him fuck her hard and soft, long and slow until she came. Her moans cling again in my ears. She fucking loved his cock.

It's too much.

"We're finished, Lindsay. You'll not see me again. I'm done with you." I jump out of the bathtub before my irritation gets the best of me, gather my belongings from the floor along with a towel, and head to the front door without looking back to see what she's doing.

I hurry with drying myself and putting on my clothes and open the door to escape from her life for good. However, a man and a woman in police uniform stop me on my way.

"We received a phone call from a Lindsay Doheny regarding an intruder," the male officer says. "Is she inside?"

I hear Lindsay speaking but don't dare look at her for the anger still boiling inside me. "I'm Lindsay Doheny," she says. "I called 9-1-1." Her voice is menacing, and I realize what a fucking situation I've gotten myself in. Lindsay won't be completely wrong if she claims I raped her. Her body must have enough bruises to prove her point along with her timely phone call.

Shit.

She might not have a bullying nature, but our breakup must have provided her with sufficient reasons for her to want to see me behind bars.

"Sir, can you please step outside with your hands on your head?" the male officer instructs.

"Sure." My heart beats faster, although it didn't have time to recover from the earlier bathroom gymnastics and the bomb Lindsay set off with her final words. Fear settles inside me as I walk out and place my hands on my head.

While the male officer searches my body, the female officer goes inside for Lindsay. "Are you okay, ma'am?"

This could be my end. Lindsay has the power to end my life with mere words. I don't hear her reply as the male officer asks me to show him a photo ID.

With trembling hands, I reach for my wallet inside the pocket of my jacket and produce my driver's license. While the officer studies it, I try to steal a glance at Lindsay, holding my breath, and see her wrapped up in a white bathrobe and talking to the other officer with her back turned against me. What is she saying? Is she mad enough to send me to jail?

"He's my ex," I hear Lindsay say. "He came to check up on me. I thought he was someone else. I couldn't see him clearly in the dark." I feel my arms loosen with relief as the anxiety abandons my body, although the female officer doesn't seem to be all that convinced by Lindsay's explanation and scans the living room with suspicious eyes.

After the female officer asks Lindsay a few questions about the specifics of my visit, she leaves the apartment and nods to her partner. Both officers eye me up and down before heading toward the elevator at the end of the hall.

I take a step toward the doorway to thank Lindsay, but her hand is already on the door, pushing it against my face. The way she's glaring at me, you'd think I attempted to kill her sister. Just before she closes it, she stops, gritting her teeth, and whispers, "Go, Ace, and never come back."

CH 9 - The Sleeping Un-Beauty

I'd be completely happy if I lived in a world where no men existed. Or at least their dicks should be chopped away for men to be able to reside in my dream world, because in ninety-nine out of a hundred cases, dick equals to problem.

It's always the dick, the root of evil and misery and the merciless opportunist. It fools us women into believing that we love the man with whom we have sex. If man and woman could fall in love without the manipulation of a dick, that'd be the true and pure love and it would never be tainted by cheating or the other issues that come with the dick.

It's disgusting, disconcerting, and belittling how much men have control over us simply because they own a dick. Burn, dicks! They should all go to hell. I'd rather have my fingers and dildos than lose myself to some dick.

Leaning against the door I've just closed against Ace's face, I drop on my butt and cover my moist face with my hands, letting the tears run freely.

I wasn't exactly happy the last few days with dirt and hunger and all, but I was getting there. Maybe in a week or so I'd be ready to take a shower by myself rather than being dragged into my own bathroom and fucked into cleanliness.

All the soaps and shampoos can't take away the dirty feeling spilling inside me now at the thought of letting that ass of a man touch me in the most tasteless way. He must have fucked a dozen women in the past few days, and I've just become another little number on his list. Yuck. I'd gladly throw up to rid myself of the dirty feeling if I had some food in my stomach.

Why did he have to come over? How in the world did he have the key to my apartment? Taylor and Adam are the only other people besides me who have a key to my place. Which means one of them is the culprit.

Since Adam is similar to me in terms of choosing violence over talking to solve problems, Taylor is the likely candidate to win the naïve-of-the-year award for asking help from Ace himself, the very reason for my self-diagnosed depression.

What am I supposed to do now? I don't feel well enough to allow food into my body. Well, I wasn't feeling well enough to allow Ace into my body either, but it didn't stop me from climaxing.

Fuck!

The best thing to do is just not to think about it. Pretend it never happened. My skin never feasted on his touch. My breasts never indulged in his roughness. My sex never pulsated around his dick. None of it was real. It was simply an hallucination, a predictable result of my severely depleted physical state.

With new conviction, I get back onto my feet and walk to my dark bedroom to go back to where I've left off in my dark life. Sleeping is good. Sleeping after drinking some cheap wine is the best. It's a pity marijuana isn't prescription-free in California. After the bathroom escapade, my mind could use a stronger form of intoxication.

I drop the bathrobe to the floor, find a t-shirt and a pair of panties to put on, and fall down on my bed face-first. But now that I'm clean, the pillow and the bed cover smell awful. Oh, and the mattress, too. In fact, I'm starting to think I'm not the only occupant on the bed, and that a few colonies of bed mites must be cohabitating beside me. I'd rather have their presence a hundred times over having Ace share the bed with me.

That motherfucker vagina-lover! He must be thinking I'm some kind of a cum-catcher for breaking into my home and fucking me senseless. Fuck him and his entire family.

My mouth is too dry, and I realize he didn't kiss me, which goes to show he lives only for his dick. Well maybe not exactly that. I run my tongue over my teeth and note the extra layer coating them. They'll need some serious brushing and cleansing for a man to be able to stomach kissing me again.

I don't want another man kissing me. I need only Ace's lips pressing against mine, probing and teasing, then his tongue sticking into my mouth. I curse myself for not caring about my mouth hygiene, at least.

Being fucked might be demeaning, but being kissed is spirit-lifting, hope-inducing, and heart-fluttering. Like watching rainbows or letting dozens of colorful balloons fly into the sky, or lying down in a garden full of flowers. I need to be kissed. And however I hate him, it has to be Ace kissing me to complete the beauty of the kiss.

Reaching for the bottle of orange juice, I gulp down nearly a quart of it. Taylor refuses to buy wine for me anymore, so I have to find solace in juices and water. I put the bottle back with its six other friends, all emptied by me. After promising myself I'll brush my teeth the next time I get out of the bed, I close my eyes for another round of sleep.

He's not coming back. This was probably the last time

I will see him, and I'm totally fine with it. My eyes moisten again with fresh tears, as if objecting to my conclusion, reminding me of the dreams I once had for Ace when we would leave everything behind us. Now that Michael is gone and there's no more threat to Ace's family, Ace has shown me his true face, ripping away all the innocent dreams I had of love.

"I'm over him," I whisper to my smelly pillow. "He's just history."

The next time I wake up, my bladder is about to explode. I slither down the bed and walk to the bathroom with eyes closed, because honestly, who needs to see the world in its ugliest form? A loud yawn overtakes me as I sit on the porcelain bowl, and I'm forced to open my eyes. Sleeping must be on the list of addictions, because the longer I sleep, the more it seems my body needs it.

I glance at my reflection in the mirror while washing my hands. My hair, now weirdly curly and tangled, is the definition of wild and will cause the hair salons to ban me as a customer.

I'll have to cut it short by myself to get rid of the impossible tangles. With my non-existent stylist talent, I'll end up giving myself the Kim Jong-un haircut and perhaps be granted citizenship in North Korea immediately for honoring their leader. Perhaps that's what I should do. Get out of the States and start a new life in a completely different country.

I hear my phone ringing in my bedroom. It's either Taylor or Zane who's calling. As surprising as it may sound, Zane hasn't given up on me and calls me almost daily to ask me out on a date. I suppose his definition of a date is more like a quick visit to his bedroom, but he's not very clear on that and keeps on blubbering about how much he wants to be with me.

I stopped answering his calls and only reply to the ones I get from my supervisor in the Marketing department. Apparently, Zane put me on unlimited sick leave to ensure my position in Hawkins Media Group. After Michael's death and the scandal Zane caused, Hawkins Media Group received a lot of attention from the public, and it seems Frat House is back on TV with more fans than it ever had.

How lovely were those days, when I could enjoy a TV show; now all my mind can think about is sleep. I'd call myself Sleeping Beauty if I had any kind of prettiness left in me.

I shrug to myself and drag my feet back to my bedroom and allow its familiar foul odor to welcome me. As I take a step through the doorway, the silhouette of a man startles me. I widen my eyes to see it's none other than Ace, and he's holding my phone in his hand.

"What are you doing here?" I stride toward him and grab my phone out of his hand.

He's sitting on the only armchair I keep in the bedroom, looking totally comfortable with his legs crossed and all. His eyes roam over my body with intent, making me aware of my bare legs beneath the short t-shirt. "You're not with Zane, are you? What ... now you've started lying?" he accuses.

Truth is for the ones who deserve it. But, I keep silent and raise my chin to look down on him with disgust. He's wearing his hair free on his shoulders today, just the way that makes my knees go weak.

Taylor's name appears on the screen of my phone as the phone starts ringing once again, and I tap on ignore to divert the call to voice mail. I'd try the police trick on Ace to get him out, but after the incident with 9-1-1, I don't think he'll take my threat seriously.

Placing his hands on the arms of the chair, he slowly ascends to his feet and stands inches before me, towering over me as if trying to scare me away by showing off his strength. Only I'm not scared. I'm pissed off.

"Have you showered today?"

Today? How much time has passed since the day he showered me? It can't be longer than a day, I guess, since my bladder wouldn't last longer without emptying itself, unless I paid a visit to the bathroom without having any memory of it.

I give my head a little shake to answer his question, lowering my eyes in embarrassment to his large chest which is concealed beneath a black t-shirt. He smells of soap mixed with a seductive hint of orange spice, as opposed to the special blend of sweat, mattress, and pillow I must be reeking of.

His muscles flex, the sight of them making my heart leap faster, and an urge to reach out and touch them and feel their strength fills my veins. He lifts his hand, pointing his finger toward the bathroom.

"Who are you? My mother?" I slowly raise my gaze to his face and allow myself a brief internal shiver in response to the anger in his eyes. My stubbornness dissolves into dust, and I spin on my heels like a dutiful soldier and head in the direction I'm ordered to go.

He follows me, keeping a small distance between us, and stops at the doorway of the bathroom. Will he come inside and watch me to make sure I'm all cleaned up? I remember I didn't get a kiss from him yesterday, or whenever it was that he visited me, and who knows when a man will kiss me again?

Although Ace expects me to hop into the shower, I stop by the sink and reach for my toothbrush, roll a generous amount of paste on it, and start brushing my teeth.

"Good idea. You smell like your last supper was your skunk roommate."

"Shut up." I gather water with my hand and throw it on his t-shirt. He jumps back, shaking his head, making tsk sounds, all the while grinning at me. My heart kicks hard against my chest at the beautiful sight of his face, all soft and relaxed.

When I'm done brushing my teeth, he points to the bathtub with his eyes. He's leaning on the doorframe, his arms crossed over his chest. Is he going to stand there and keep on watching me?

"Go, wait in the living room." I move forward and close the door. Taking my t-shirt and panties off, I toss them on the floor, run the water, and get in the bathtub.

Why is he back? Didn't he say we were finished? Have I dreamed it all? I fill my hand with body wash and smear it around my body. The soreness between my legs is proof that none of it was the result of my imagination.

As I go under the water to rinse the foam off my body, the curtain is pulled open, and Ace is standing before me totally naked.

"Don't say no," he says with one intent clear in his eyes; to screw me, and to screw me good. Before I can utter a word, he steps in behind me and twirls me around to face him. He stares at my lips expectantly, and I gulp, unsure of what to do.

I want to be kissed so badly, the acute urgency of it is giving me physical pain. I feel I won't be able to breathe if I don't get a taste of his lips. He can fuck me all he wants, but I won't let him get away without a heart-melting kiss. I fucking brushed my teeth for it and he'll be a damned fool if he deprives me of the only balm to my hurting heart.

He continues staring at me but doesn't move a limb, perhaps waiting for me to make the first move.

"You shouldn't have expected a serious commitment from a man who runs a brothel, right? I mean, come on. It just defies the logic in every sense."

How can I initiate anything with a man who used me and treated me like a piece of shit? Am I such a masochist?

My lips tighten; my eyes close, and a wave of sadness settles in my heart. "I can't." I start crying. Ace pulls me, letting our bodies crash against each other, and lifts my chin up to his face.

"You broke my heart, Lindsay. You ruined me with no possibility of recovery." With that, he launches forward and captures my lips, and gives me the kiss I've been yearning for all this time. His hands are tight on my cheeks, then around my neck. His lips knead mine with both love and hatred, and I open up for him, longing for the taste of his mouth. His tongue plunges in to wrestle with mine. The taste of him is so sweet, like ripe strawberries, and I savor him without caring about the problems between us.

I'm done with being one and alone by myself. I'm ready to be one with him again, with both lust and love, to become his again and to make him mine, despite the presence of other women in his life. I lock my arms around his waist to pull him closer, unable to do anything else but accept any comfort and pain our reunion might give me.

The rough edges of his body, the curves of his round buttocks, the fiery warmth of his skin, and the feeling of his hard cock poking at my belly make me dizzy with desire. Perhaps any man who knows a thing or two about female orgasm can make me climax, but only Ace can inflict lust in me so high it sets off powerful wild fires inside me.

Just when our kiss is deepening, he draws back, taking me out of the dream I was losing myself in, and looks down at me with hooded eyes. "I thought you were a panther," he says, leaving me confused with his words. "But, I was wrong. You're a snake. A vicious, merciless snake. You inject your venom with one bite, and game over for your prey. No amount of fucking you can take out your poison."

My lips curl up, revealing perhaps the only genuine smile I've had in weeks. "Does that mean you'll come back for more?"

"Honestly, I wish it didn't, but once bitten, always smitten." He smashes his mouth back against mine, picks me up like he did yesterday, and wraps my legs around his hips, crushing me against his body with his tight hold. I'd rather have pain while in his arms than no feeling at all without him. I lock my arms around his neck and make room for him to adjust his cock between us.

I want him. I need him, apparently more than food, and I crave to be filled by him again. "You're my poison, Ace. You're my only poison. Fuck me and make me forget."

He slides the head of his cock from my clit down to my entrance, augmenting my desire for him tenfold, and swirls it without entering me. "Do you desire Zane?"

No. I want to tell him, 'no,' but then I remember his other women and decide to torture him with my silence.

"Answer me." He eases his cock inside me slowly, making me feel every inch of him as it stretches me out.

"No." I bite my lip to stop the moan tearing up from the depths of my throat. "But I won't say you're the only man I desire when you keep on fucking other women."

"Haven't you been listening, woman? I'm smitten by you and only you. You're the only woman I can think of fucking. You took the allure of other women completely out of me."

"But, you said—"

"I lied."

"You didn't sleep with anyone else?"

"No."

"How about the blonde in your office?"

"I was only trying to take revenge on you. Nothing happened between her and me."

I could ask for more of an explanation but his dick, as always, is doing a fantastic job of shutting off my brain, and I give myself to him without any reservations and move my hips up and down along his thick length to get more of him.

He's mine, whether he likes it or not. He belongs to me, just like I belong to him.

He murmurs my name over and over again like a child who has learned a new word. I'd voice my love for him if I had any control over my tongue, or my body for that matter, as a wave of orgasm approaches at full speed.

I moan and freeze, the only thing I can manage to do when it hits me and an electrical charge goes from my core through my body.

"How many times did you come with him?" Ace whispers in my ear, and I realize I'm resting my head on his shoulder, tightly grasping his shoulders.

What a great question to ruin the moment. "What? I don't remember."

"How many times?"

Sighing loudly, I mumble, "Once with his hands, once with him inside of me."

I tilt my head back to glance at his face. My answer

doesn't surprise him, but it doesn't calm him down either. "At least he didn't fuck your mouth."

I blink and swallow, unsure if I should correct him or make him believe what he wants to believe.

"Did you suck him, too? Tell me the truth."

"The following day, he forced me in the elevator. I ... had no choice."

"There's always a choice. Now go down and suck me off." He pulls out of me and drops me onto my feet, gesturing with his chin for me to kneel. How can he claim there's always a choice when he leaves me no way to take away his jealousy other than going down on him? At least the water is drizzling on his hard cock so I won't have to lick my own juices.

Impeccably clean or smeared in my juices, his cock is the only cock that makes my mouth water. How I could hate a dick this hard, thick, and delicious, suddenly perplexes me. Or is its charm, a part of its manipulative tricks? Perhaps yes, but I don't care about it anymore. It's all mine to relish.

He growls and takes a step back to balance himself when I take all of him into my mouth without a warning. "Fuck, Lindsay. Slow down. I want to enjoy it." He fists his hands into my hair to push me back.

I grit my teeth onto his flesh to caution him to back off and let me do it the way I want to. His hands loosen—obviously, he's got my message—but his body stiffens, perhaps to gain some control against my intense licking.

Grabbing the base of his cock with one hand, his balls with the other, I lick him to my heart's content, swirling my tongue on the head of his cock each time my lips reach up, alternating between fast and slow, rough and gentle, moaning and purring to show him I too get pleasure out of it…immense pleasure.

He comes with an explosion, without warning, and pushes my head against his cock as it pulses out its last drops inside my mouth.

"How could I go so long without this?" he murmurs while sliding out of me. He helps me to my feet and washes me and himself with lots of body wash. We grab towels and hurry back to my bedroom.

While I dry myself, he goes through my closet and drawers and picks out a red, transparent blouse, a black, knee-length skirt, a black brassier, and black panties for me.

"Put these on. I'm taking you out for dinner."

"I'm not hungry."

"You looked very hungry to me back in the bathroom." His lips curve up, revealing his pearly whites.

"Haha. I don't think I can eat anything after having lived on wine and orange juice for two weeks."

"I don't expect you to eat a steak. You can start with soup and see what else you have an appetite for."

"I guess I can try that."

"I can't believe you did that to yourself."

I shrug and slide into the panties and the bra. When we're both fully clothed, he finds a comb on my vanity table, sits on the chair, and orders me to sit on the floor in front of him. He's taking up the challenge to tame my wild hair, and I appreciate the enthusiasm, but there's no way he'll be done with my hair before next year.

He starts cursing with the first strand of hair, then finds the solution in a bottle of coconut oil that I've been neglecting for a very long time. I have to laugh at his choice but don't voice any of the dozens of jokes running through my head about Zane and his allergy to coconut oil.

"That'll make him stay away from you for good," he says as he applies a generous amount of oil on my hair. "Why the fuck didn't I think about this before?"

"He can try all he wants to gain my attention, I don't care about him." I turn my head around and look up at him. "You're the only one for me. It's been so for a long time."

"Why then did you turn to him for help? Didn't you think I'm as able and clever as him?"

"Noooo! That's not it. I looked for you, but then I panicked when I couldn't find you anywhere. I had to do something quick. I heard Edward talking to his assistant about bringing more men in case you weren't willing to give him what he wanted. I wanted to protect you. I didn't want you to suffer, and Zane had a solution."

"You and I obviously have a different perception of pain. I'd rather have Edward and all his men fuck me than watch Zane ..."

"No. Are you crazy?"

"Yeah, crazy for you. You'll not ask help from him anymore. You'll come to me as the first and only person to solve any issues you have."

I sigh in defiance.

"I'm serious, Lindsay. If you want this to work, I'll be the main person in your life, as you already are in mine." He continues working on my hair, combing through the tangles one by one with patience and gentleness only he can muster.

"How about Taylor? You can't seriously expect me to put you above her."

"Will you ever comply with any of my wishes without questioning me?" he asks and tugs at my hair so I face him. "Will I ever hear a 'yes' from your mouth without having to convince you?"

"I guess not."

He shakes his head in mock disbelief and ducks to press his lips gently against mine.

"Come on up. Your hair is ready." He holds my hand to help me up, and I head directly to the mirror to see his handiwork.

"What the hell did you do to my hair?" I gape at the oily hair stuck to my scalp like second skin. "I look horrible."

"You're exaggerating. It doesn't look worse than a minute ago."

I run the comb through my hair in an attempt to give it some volume without success and then wind up tying it into a low bun behind my head. "Now I look like a flamenco dancer."

Ace laughs, sneaking his arms around my waist from behind, and hugs me against his torso. "Come on. Let's get some food into your stomach. Your ass feels shrunk. I want it back to its form before the end of the month."

"Huh. Here I thought you were worrying about my wellbeing."

He gives me a scorching smile with a seductive glance down at my body and holds my hand to guide me out. We drive in his car to a Chinese restaurant and order noodle soup.

With the first spoon, I start crying for the inability of my palate to detect any taste. I might not be a professional in the food industry or even a foodist, but the fear of not being able to enjoy the taste of the food is just too much to bear.

Ace laughs at me and points out that he ordered the waitress not to add any flavor or spice into my soup when he left for the restroom. I ask for salt and lemon to spice up my dish and sigh with relief when my taste buds register the distinct sour taste.

To my surprise Taylor and Adam join us for the dessert, actually to ruin the dessert for Ace, because both start preaching about my wellbeing, adding threats from burning down Ace's establishment, dirtying his name in the media, to cutting off his fingers. The last one is from Adam, and I bet he means another part of Ace's body but is gentlemanly enough not to voice it in front of ladies.

Then, they inform us of the news about Taylor's pregnancy, which I should have noticed from the growth of her belly. I start crying again and hug Taylor. It looks like a life without real food and Ace has turned me into a cry baby.

At the end of the dinner, while walking back to the restaurant's parking lot, Adam pulls Ace aside, I guess, to make sure he understood the dangers awaiting him if he breaks my heart one more time.

Ace and I drive back to my apartment, and as soon as I open the door, the heavy smell of dirt hits me like a blow and turns my stomach upside down. Ace wasn't lying when he joked about me hosting a skunk as my roommate.

We stay only half an hour to gather some of my personal belongings and clothes to use and wear at Ace's place. Taking advantage of the unlivable conditions of my apartment, Ace asks me to move in with him.

As much as I love him, I'm not ready to combine our lives just yet, but I can't for the life of me stay another night in my place, so I take his offer until I find a professional cleaner brave enough to go through my apartment.

I should be cautious not to allow my heart any more disaster and take Ace's promises lightly, but it's impossible not to start dreaming about a future together with Ace when he's stripping naked before me in his bedroom, his eyes locked on mine, first his shirt, then his jeans, and oh my.

He's hard again, and seeing the desire flaring up in his eyes, I get wet instantly. His skin glows golden despite the dim light, his blue eyes beaming like a flashlight. His sturdy body is designed to fuck, there's no denying that.

He slides between the bed sheets, tugs them up only until his abs, his cock making a tent beneath the silk fabric. I swallow and suck my bottom lip, smiling, as he pats at the space next to him, the space I thought was mine until he kicked me out of his life. Can I handle one more rejection? It doesn't take a psychiatrist to know the answer is no...that simple.

"Take them all off. I want you naked," he purrs, lust dripping off his plump lips.

My sex pulsates with his words and his I-will-fuck-you-hard-till-you-pass-out stare. I squeeze my thighs, unable to do anything else, and start working on my blouse. My body is under his spell and I can't just get the fuck out of his life, even though that'd be the sound thing to do.

His eyes follow my fingers like his life depends on the outcome. I shrug out of my blouse and then my bra, already panting with lust. Tugging my skirt and panties down together, I stand fully naked before him and watch his face harden with intense desire.

He lifts the sheet for me, revealing to me once more his cock, intimidating and ready to fuck, and I lie next to him, facing him, our bodies merely touching each other. He bucks his hips and I suck in a deep breath as the tip of it slides between my legs, directly stimulating my clit.

"Open up that sweet pussy for me."

"I'm scared."

He smiles. "Of my cock?"

"Of you."

"You? Scared of me?"

"Of what you can do to me. I can't survive another blow. You straight out kicked me out of your life."

"I won't do it again as long as you stay away from Zane." He moves forward and above me and impales me with one easy move. I cry out with shock, and get a hold of his shoulder as he plunges his tongue into my mouth. His eyes never leave mine as he fucks me, as if searching for a hint of insincerity.

Though the intensity of desire is heating my flesh, burning up my insides more with each stroke of his cock, my mind won't allow me to let go and reach the climax, as it's only fucking, no love involved. No kissing, no words of admiration, or affection when I clearly showed him my vulnerability.

"...as long as you stay away from Zane."

Why is our relationship conditioned upon Zane? Does he want me only because his brother is after me? Is it a way for him to get his revenge on his brother? Is he using me? I'd rather be a means to blow his nuts than have him using me to get back at his brother.

I close my eyes, because tears are stinging them, and turn my face to the side, all my desire for him vanishing quickly.

He drops on his elbows on either side of me, peers into my face, his head close to mine. "What is it? Am I hurting you?"

Yes.

"Talk to me."

I shake my head no and allow a loud sob to escape my mouth. He slows down his speed and presses his temple against my head.

"I can't do this," I find myself saying. "I can't continue without knowing where we stand."

"I don't understand. I want to be with you, and as far as I can tell, you want that too. I thought I made myself clear on that."

"Why do you want me?" Because of Zane?

He stops, but continues keeping his penis inside me. "Because I can't pass a day without thinking about you. I'm pining after you like a hormonal teenager. Because the day you walked out of my life, I thought that was it for me—that I didn't have anything else to live for. I was a living death. I've never had a woman who dazzled me and shut off my brain completely like you do. I even wanted to fuck your brains out while you smelled like shit." I bite my lips to stifle a laugh. "I'd give my entire fortune to find out what exactly makes you so special in my eyes that I can't fucking breathe at the thought of another man fucking you, but I'm ready to leave it in the past because not having you in my life hurts so much fucking more than what you and Zane did to me."

Either he's a natural actor like Zane, or his words are coming straight from his heart. I turn my face to him and lock my teary eyes on his. "That sounds like love to me."

"May be." I see him crook his head to the side and flash me a teasing smile. "Want to figure it out together?"

I melt down as his eyes stare at me as if I'm one of the wonders of the world. It's a far cry from any stare any man has ever given me. More tears well up in my eyes. He wipes them away from my temples, his thumbs gentle, affectionate, and ducks down to kiss me, to own my lips, to convince me of the truthfulness of his semi-love declaration, sliding in and out of me with slow moves until my mind surrenders and lets go.

I don't quite realize when the words "I love you" slip

out of my mouth and only notice it when he crushes his lips to mine, then pulls away to say it back to me. "I love you, Lindsay."

He owns me, my heart, my soul, my body, and now we've made it official.

CH 10 - The Test

We open up our deep feelings, spend the night loving and making love to each other; however, love isn't enough if not accompanied by trust and respect.

The next morning, I slide out of the bed, while Ace is sleeping, head to the kitchen to grab a bite and tea before work. After a quick shower, I find Ace still sound asleep in his bed. I blow dry my hair and put on a pair of black slacks and a gray blouse, all set to resume my work at the marketing department of HMG, now under Zane's ownership.

Just when I unlock the door, I hear Ace call my name in a very sexy tone that makes my toes curl in my shoes. I leave my jacket and the satchel that carries my laptop on the table and stride back to the bedroom. His expression goes from dazzled to confused and then ends in irritated.

"Why aren't you naked and in bed with me?" His lust-filled eyes wander over the curves of my body, and he lifts the bed cover to invite me in beside him and also to show me his morning hard-on.

"I have to go to work," I explain, but my feet fail me and I end up sitting on the edge of the bed.

He frowns at me, then smiles at my easy submission. "What work?" His hand covers mine and drags it over his hips and when I spread my fingers, he presses my palm against the head of his cock. His skin is hot and infuses acute desire into my body. I take a sharp breath, sinking my teeth into my lip, and squeeze my thighs together to control my urges.

"At the Hawkins Media Group. The work is waiting for me."

"You didn't seem to be bothered by it yesterday or the day before for that matter." His hand closes over mine, mine over his cock, and we massage it with slow but firm strokes. He growls his readiness to take me right there and then, his obvious desire drawing a soft moan from me. His hooded eyes silently convey what he's planning on doing to me.

"Now I have a clear perspective about what I want to do."

Ace throws his other arm up to cover his eyes as he bucks his hips up against my hand, his hand harder on mine. "Oh, yeah? What do you want to do?"

I climb up and kneel on the bed, bowing my head down to his hips. "First this," I say and yank his hand away to free mine and curl my fingers around his thick shaft.

"Oh, boy. What else?"

A smile curves my lips while I let my tongue sweep across the head of his member. My hand strokes his growing erection the rough way he likes, and he responds to my assault with curses rolling out of his restrained lips. More saliva gathers in my mouth at the taste of his salty arousal, and I close my lips around his thickness, sliding more of him inside my mouth.

"You're not going anywhere today," he hisses, his voice coated with lust. "I'd like to spend my day in that sweet mouth of yours."

I take him in deeper till his hardness hits my throat and feel his thick vein pulsate against my tongue, my sex throbbing with the need to be filled again. He won't last long, much less a day as he claims. My lips stroke him with long, pressuring moves, and he erupts unexpectedly and with a thick load.

"So much for spending your day in my mouth," I joke as I rush to the bathroom to wash up my face before his seed reaches down to my shirt.

"That was just an appetizer," he yells after me with laughter.

His eyes are closed when I come back to the bedroom. I tiptoe to his side in case he's fallen asleep and lean down to give him a kiss.

"You're not going anywhere," he murmurs and catches my wrist. His eyes open and stare back at me with anger. "I don't want you near Zane. Remember our deal?"

"Oh, Ace. He's not any danger to me or to us. He doesn't have any power over me. If anything, I hold the key to his incarceration for forcing me to have sex with him."

Rather than calming him down, my words escalate the fury in his eyes, but he lets go of my hand and sits up straight in the bed. "He won't give up on you."

"It doesn't matter. I can handle him. I promise." I circle my arms around his neck and press my lips against his.

"You taste like cum," he murmurs between kisses. "I like it."

I pull away from him and gather my purse. "Let's meet for lunch. I know a great, little café a few blocks away from my work."

I leave and hurry for my car. My colleagues welcome me back with shockingly warm words while I drop my purse in the drawer of my desk. I'd prefer starting straight with work, but I'll have to see Zane first to let him know

I'm back.

He's taken Michael's office, but instead of Julie, a young, blonde girl is occupying the ante-room of the office and phones Zane to announce my arrival. Zane meets me at the door with his arms wide open for me.

I glare at him, wishing my eyes had lasers so I could burn his cock alive. "You can't possibly think I'm going to hug you after all the things you did to me."

Ignoring my comment, he walks up to me, making me spring back in disgust under the curious eyes of the new secretary. "I've missed you so much."

"If you get anywhere near me, I'm filing sexual harassment charges against you." My stomach twists as the scent of his cologne hits me, reminding me of the depraved minutes I had with him.

"Why are you cold to me again? Ace left you. What's holding you back from being with me?"

"Would you want me to leave?" the secretary asks, possibly shocked out of her system for seeing her boss begging a woman for attention.

"No." I urge her to stay so I won't have to be alone with Zane. "I just came here to let you know that I am back to work and will stay until I complete the contract I signed with the marketing department. But, don't get your hopes high. I'm not single. Ace and I are back together."

"Lindsay, no. You're making a huge mistake. He's going to break your heart," Zane screams as I turn around and stalk out of the anteroom.

I pay a half-hour visit to the director of the marketing department to get information about the new project that I'll be working on and head back to my desk. Except for the minor fact that I report to Zane, my life is how I've always wanted it to be, with a wonderful boyfriend and a job I love. No one is threatening to hurt me or my family, and I don't have to worry about my finances.

Opening up the file of the new project on my computer, I immerse myself into the world of numbers and computations and allow my mind for the first time to fully worry about one thing and one thing only— delivering the project error-free and on time.

About eleven a.m., my phone rings, Ace's name flashing on its screen. My heart hammers against my chest as I answer it. "Hello there," I reply in a low, flirty tone. "Already miss me?"

"Lindsay, I can't do it," Ace says. "I can't pretend to be fine while you continue working for Zane."

A sudden chill of fear runs through my back. "We talked about this." I get up to step out to a secluded corner to have some privacy.

"No amount of talking can convince me. I can't go on while he's so close to you."

"But, what do you want?" I ask, fearing his answer.

"You know what I want. I explained it clearly last night. I'll be with you, have a relationship and all, as long as you stay away from Zane. That was the deal."

Frustration gets the best of me. I'm tired of doing what others expect me to do. Why can't they just let me be and live my life the way I deem appropriate? Even Ace, who claims to have feelings for me, won't respect my decisions. "Ace, please. Let's talk about it later."

"There's no later, Lindsay. I want you to come home now or…"

"Or, what? You'll finish it? You'll break up with me? Are you so egotistical that you won't allow me to work at the job I love? Is that what you are trying to say?"

"Yes."

Yes? Short, to the point, and hurtful like a snakebite. Tears gather in my eyes. This can't be happening. Just when I thought everything was in perfect harmony… "Don't ask me to choose. Please, I love you, but I won't feel comfortable in our relationship knowing you place your insecurities above my happiness."

"Sorry, but it can't work the way you want it."

"It can and it will. Just give me some time to prove it to you. I really like the project I'm working on. My supervisor is a great mentor, and I don't really want to leave so early into my contract."

"No, Lindsay. You'll have to choose—either me or your work."

"If you put it that way…I'll stay with my work. At least it doesn't demand me to choose between my happiness and its own selfish wishes," I say heartbroken, hoping my move will get him back down.

"Is that your final word?"

"Yes." My answer can be short and hurtful too. I open my mouth to continue but I'm confronted with the dial tone. Has he just hung up on me?

I dial him back over and over again, and each time his answering machine picks up. I'm not living the same chasing-after-Ace torture all over again. I can't do it. I don't have any strength left in me to fight to amend our broken relationship.

I allow myself a few minutes of crying and grieving over the short-lived bliss I had with Ace, hiding out in the restroom until lunchtime. The rest of the day goes in a blur, and promptly at five p.m., I gather my purse and head out.

I don't even have a place to go since my apartment is still in an un-livable condition. Taylor's home is my only option although the last thing I want from her is to worry about me. She receives me with a warm hug and silent support anyway, doesn't ask about the reason for my non-stop crying, and lies next to me on the bed until I sleep.

I remember to have a shower and eat during the second post-Ace period and dedicate myself to work. After all, I chose it over the man I love. I'd better be great at it. As much as my performance at work blooms and blossoms, I curl in my bed in Taylor's guestroom in the evenings, hugging a picture of Ace and me together and crying myself to sleep.

Zane sends me three to four emails a day for a chance to meet me in private. I stopped reading them a long time ago and directly send them to trash.

Two weeks into my breakup with Ace, I receive a brief email from Philip, the head of the marketing department, inviting me to his office for a meeting. It's odd because I never see him unless there's a department meeting where everyone on the team is required to be present; not just me.

Is he going to fire me despite my best efforts to deliver high-quality projects? My immediate supervisor never complained about mistakes in my computations, but my miserable attitude and my immense need to be alone might be the reasons getting in my way to be perceived as a successful employee in the eyes of the executives.

I fist my hands to keep them from trembling as I enter Philip's office. He's an average-height and athletically built man in his late forties and doesn't usually radiate a friendly energy, much like me, but he's a high-level executive whose job is to emit fear and coldness, and I'm a subordinate who should probably be giving away heaps of smiles and praises as a part of my work duties.

"Miss Doheny, please have a seat." He lifts his hand to show me the chair before his desk. "We'll go over some important details regarding your appointment in the marketing department."

Oh, God. My appointment? Can this be Zane's doing? He must have gotten tired of chasing after me and now wants me out.

I nod and hesitantly take my seat. Philip occupies himself for some time with typing on his computer completely oblivious to my near-fainting state of mind.

"We'll start in a minute," he says when I shift in my chair as a way to show him my discomfort. I hear the door open but don't turn, thinking it's his secretary carrying coffee for him.

By the way, I realize he hasn't offered me any drink. I'm definitely getting fired. Oh, well. No boyfriend, no job. I should have known good things in life don't last long—at least not in my life.

When the secretary takes too long to show her face, I turn around and am startled to see Zane standing a few feet behind me.

"We'll be having the meeting with Mr. Hawkins," Philip says.

I narrow my eyes at Zane with anger. I won't give him the satisfaction to fire me for some idiotic reasons and most certainly won't go down without a fight or a punch in his face.

He gives me a smile that is strangely warm and reassuring. Is that the way he fires his employees? It's hard to take a man whose body I saw fully naked seriously, even if he holds power over my career.

"Do you have headphones?" Zane asks Philip, causing a questioning look to form on his face. Without prompting for an explanation, Philip calls his secretary and asks her to bring headphones. "Put them on while Lindsay and I talk," Zane orders and Philip complies.

"You didn't want to come to me." Zane drags a chair

close to me and sits beside me, his knee brushing mine.

I jerk my leg away as if touched by fire and eye Philip suspiciously. "For a good reason."

"He's gone. It's time to move on."

I breathe out my frustration and cross my arms over my chest, shaking my head to his nonsense.

"He's not coming back. In fact, I heard he's started dating someone else. Why don't you do the same and consider giving me a chance?"

My head turns sharply to face him. "No, he didn't." He can't move on so easily. He can't be seeing another woman so soon after our breakup. I feel blood draining out of me. My arms go loose on my chest.

"I heard it from Chloe. He's seeing a friend of hers."

"Enough already." I lift my hand to put an end to his torture. I'd rather be kept in the dark about Ace's romantic adventures.

"On the other hand, I haven't been with another woman since you, and I won't until I am convinced that there is absolutely no way for us to be together."

"Then you can start seeing someone else right now, because there's absolutely no way in this world or any other for you and me to be together. My answer is definite, Zane. I don't want to be with you, not now, not ever."

"Ouch."

"Yeah, truth hurts."

"But, you said you were attracted to me in the beginning. I saw it in your eyes on those first days we met. You can't fall for me again?"

"No, Zane. It's impossible. The window of opportunity is gone. Ace is all I can think about right now, and it won't change for a long time."

"I can wait."

I shake my head.

"If Ace hadn't stolen you away, if I had owned my emotions from earlier on…"

"There's no point in delving into possible scenarios based on if's. Things happened and we can't change them anymore. It's better if you come to terms with it just the way I have to come to terms with the fact that Ace has moved on. As much as it hurts, it's best for both of us."

"If only you weren't this stubborn," Zane adds, his voice laced with disappointment, his head falling down on his chest.

"But I am, and you can't change that either."

He stands, gives Philip and me a little nod to signal the end of the meeting, and stalks out of the office. Philip wishes me a good day at work and dismisses me. I hurry to the first bathroom and cry silently until I convince myself that my breakup with Ace is final and he doesn't deserve more tears from me.

My misery continues for another two weeks until I realize how stupid both Ace and I have been for throwing away a beautiful relationship just like that. And there's only one person who can fix it.

Zane.

I can't believe I'll need him again, but this time he won't have any power over me to coerce me into forced sex—just the contrary.

I make a surprise visit to his office, half-expecting to catch him between the legs of some cat-walk model. He lifts his head from his computer to glance at me with an astounded expression. "You, here?"

"Hi, Zane. How are you? I brought you a croissant and coffee." I set the beverage cup and the paper bag on his desk. He stares at them with suspicion before going ahead and grabbing the cup of coffee.

"You're being nice to me. Wait a minute. Did you put poison in the coffee?"

His silly question elicits an unexpected smile from me. Skipping the chair, I hop on the edge of his desk and look down on him, while he takes a small sip from his drink without waiting for my response. "You're drinking it?"

"Yeah, I assume you wouldn't want me dead just yet."

"Why is that?" My smile grows wider.

"Who else will chase after you if I'm gone? Every woman needs an admirer, and you're damned lucky to have an awesome one like me." He leans forward to get the paper bag and takes a big bite out of the chocolate croissant.

"Uh...about that... I need an official statement from you that you'll no longer have any romantic or sexual interest in me."

"Excuse me?" He chokes on the croissant bite and grabs the hot beverage for aide.

"You heard me right. We don't need an attorney or a notary, but you'll do it in front of your family."

"Lindsay, I'm not giving up on you."

Dropping the smile, I stare straight into his eyes with a stern gaze. "You are. It's time to let go. If you don't do it willingly, I'll have to file sexual harassment charges against you, and I promise it won't be pretty. I have a strong case. You can lose everything you worked so hard for—your job, your freedom, even your money. Who do you think will take over HMG if you're in jail? Let me answer it for you: Ace. You lost me to him; are you ready to lose the company that should belong to you to him as well? Think about it."

Placing the croissant and the cup on the desk, he leans back against his chair, gathering up his leg on his other knee. "Why are you so sure you're going to win? It's your word against mine."

"I have Laila to testify for me. And, I have the video recordings of the forceful oral sex in the elevator." I fish out a USB flash-drive from my pocket and throw it to his hand.

He catches it in the air and hooks it up to his computer. "Fuck. Why didn't I take care of it?"

"Yeah, even a perfectionist like you can fail to get rid of all the traces."

He gathers his head between his hands, silently watching the recording of his filthy performance. "God, does that mean I won't see that ass naked again?"

"Fuck you." I launch forward and unhook the drive to end the near-porn show. "Look, I don't want any more than you do to show it to anyone, but you can bet your ass I'll not shy away from using it if you don't get your act together and do as I want."

"You're impossible."

"You got that right. So, do we have a deal?"

"Yeah, whatever."

"I expect you at Chloe's place tonight at six," I instruct. "Be there on time, not a minute late. Understood?"

He nods, rolling his eyes in an exaggerated way.

Feeling glad to having sorted it out, I return my friendly smile to him and pat him on the shoulder. "Now that you officially have no feelings for me, I'm looking forward to working for you."

He tilts his head to glance at my hand. As soon as I notice his lips are approaching my skin, I yank my hand away and jump down from his desk. "Keep your shit together. I won't be forgiving next time."

Although I'd very much like to burn the recording of those evil minutes with Zane in the elevator, I keep the flash-drive on me and a copy of it in a safe place as a protection against Zane.

After my visit to Zane, I call up Chloe to make sure she's invited Ace over for the dinner she and I planned together. I can tell from the clear reluctance in her voice that she's not on board about Ace and I getting back together, but she's at least agreed on organizing the dinner for me to have a chance to talk with him. I guess she's feeling indebted to me for having tried to save her.

I'm about to see Ace for the first time after weeks, and the first question that comes to my mind is what I should wear. At times like this, I wish Edrick hadn't ran away after the Michael scandal and was here to help me out with his unique talent in finding the right clothes to bring out the usually absent sexiness of my body.

I ask for help from my sister. Rather than spending bags of money to find the perfect dress for me, she lends me a wine-red, short-sleeved, pencil, V-neck dress that gathers up my boobs and buttocks nicely. Perhaps so nicely that Zane won't be able to keep his promise and will shamelessly flirt with me in front of Ace, and my plan will backfire, and I'll lose Ace for good.

My perfectly manicured nails end up bitten up on my way to Chloe's apartment. Zane arrives before me, waiting for me at the reception of the building where Chloe lives. He blows a long whistle, eliciting whispered curses from me

The whole evening will blow up in my face. I can see it clearly now. Zane won't stop his irritating teases, which will only prove to Ace that he was right with his insecurities about me working for Zane.

I glower at Zane, now feeling more hopeless than anything else, and threaten him with the lawsuit one last time, because honestly I don't have any more patience left in me to tolerate his foolish pursuit.

"All right, all right." His hands rise up to his chest in a defensive way. "No woman is worth spending time in jail."

"You got that right."

I keep my distance from him as we enter the elevator, fighting with myself not to think about the last time I was alone in an elevator with him. I should just skip the dinner and go ahead with the lawsuit. It'll save me time and heartache.

I note an unusual cheerfulness in Chloe as she welcomes us, hugging me, then Zane at the doorway. I hear Ace's voice from afar and nearly lose all my senses. Both Zane and I fall behind Chloe as she walks us to the dining room. Ace's eyes are the first thing I see, and I nearly melt. He stares at me with a shocked expression, the blues of his eyes twinkling with warmth and amazement.

"I'm glad you could come in time to meet Ace's new girlfriend." Chloe's words shoot like sharp arrows into my chest, and I move my gaze over to the brunette sitting next to Ace.

My mind can't register anything about her except for her hand possessively lying on Ace's shoulder. I come close to collapsing on the floor, and Zane comes to my rescue, catching me by my elbow.

He wasn't lying about Ace having a girlfriend, and Chloe graciously forgot to mention this little detail to me. What's the point in trying to convince Ace about Zane's loss of interest in me if he already has someone else in his life?

"Unfortunately, I won't be staying for the dinner," Zane says. I glance up at him to see worry lines hardening his otherwise playful features. His lips curl up into a painful smile that doesn't quite reach his eyes. His eyes flick to Chloe before landing on Ace. "I just came for a few minutes to say in front of all of you that I'm no longer interested in Lindsay. I set my eyes on her a long time ago, but now I realize her heart belongs to Ace and she will never give in to my advances. She forced me into coming here to say all this in front of you, but I don't need any coercing to grasp that she and I have no future together." He then turns to me and reaches for my hands, holding them in a tight hold. "I wish you good luck. I hope we can still stay friends."

"Thank you," I whisper to him, feeling sorry for the sadness dominating his face.

"No need to thank me. I just needed to see your face when you looked at him to realize it's a lost game for me. I'm sorry for the pain I caused you. I just thought I could have a chance with you. But, well. Good luck." He leans down to give me a quick kiss on the cheek before hurrying outside.

Ace keeps his intense gaze trained on me for a long moment after Zane is gone. No one dares to speak until Ace's girlfriend breaks the silence. "Did I get it right? Is she in love with you?" She points her index finger at me then at Ace, and Ace nods, his eyes still holding mine captive. "Are you...in love with her, too?"

Ace doesn't answer, which, in itself, is an answer—at least to me. The mesmerized way he looks at me, mirroring my own stare, is clear proof that his heart is still beating for me and that he's using this girl to get over me...without success.

"I love you, Ace," I whisper.

"This is totally awkward." Ace's girlfriend pushes her chair to stand and throws the napkin to the table. "You know how to reach me if you want," she says to Ace and strolls out of the dining room. Chloe follows her out, leaving me alone with Ace.

Ace is as always breathtaking, and I wish nothing but to mold myself against the firm curves of his muscles. "Oh, Ace. I miss you so much."

He doesn't speak or move, doesn't reveal any hint for me to guess what he must be thinking.

"Don't you have anything to say?" I ask, hoping to get an answer from him now.

"I need time to let all of it sink in," are the only words he mutters before striding out of the living room, leaving me completely alone and lonely without him. I collapse on the floor, no longer fighting against the tears.

Ace takes his time to evaluate this new information— when I say time, I mean weeks. Just when I start thinking he's decided to stay with his new girlfriend, he surprises me with red roses on a lazy afternoon at Taylor's home.

"They're beautiful," I say, filling my lungs with their sweet scent, and offer him the chair beside mine in Taylor's garden.

"Not as beautiful as you." He reaches up and caresses my cheek with his index finger before settling on the chair.

Hugging the roses, I sit back in my chair and bury my nose in them, my body on high alert for Ace's unexpected visit. His hand moves up, the tip of his finger stroking my leg as he inches up to my hand and fondles it inside his palm. My heart throbs in my ears.

He doesn't need words to relay to me his decision. He's come to take me back.

"You took a lot of time," I say, enjoying the feeling of my hand inside his, but not confident enough to look him in the eye.

"I needed to be sure."

"Are you sure now?"

"Yes."

I pull away from the flowers and turn to the ocean-blue eyes that I lost myself in long ago. "No more breakups?"

He shakes his head.

"No other woman?"

"There has never been another woman since the day I met you."

My eyebrows arch up. "How about the girl at Chloe's dinner party?"

"Chloe set me up with her. I never planned anything more than a couple of friendly dates with her. She could never take your place. No one can."

Tears push their way to my eyes. "Shall I believe that?"

He replies with a smile and a nod, and I drop the roses on the table and throw myself into his arms, unable to keep the tears back.

"I love you," I whisper. "More than you can ever imagine."

His hands curl around my face, his hot breath brushing my skin, and he stares at me as if making sure I'm real and before him. Our lips find each other with urgency, and I open my mouth for him to finally get a taste of the only flavor I'm designed to cherish.

"Oh, God, I miss you so much, I could fuck you right now," he murmurs to my mouth.

A deep, guttural throat-clearing, and Ace and I part and turn to see Adam and Taylor looking down on us; Taylor with a melting expression on her face, Adam glowering.

"Not in my backyard," Adam growls at us a few feet away from my chair. Ace pushes to his feet, taking my hand into his, and hauls me out, nodding at Taylor and

Adam before we leave.

We drive to the closest shopping mall and park in the parking lot. I can barely contain my excitement and desire as he pulls me over to his lap, ripping my panties and shoving his thick member straight inside of me. Our lips fight for a reunion, our tongues for dominance. Breathless and panting, I press my body against his with the yearning to imprint him into my skin, into my soul.

When we come only seconds after one another, warm tears moisten our cheeks, his and mine mingled on our skin. I taste love on his lips, smell hot, melting desire on his skin, hear my heartbeat on his chest, his on mine.

He is worth waiting for. Not just the last weeks, but my whole life before him. He is worth the tests I had to undergo, the ordeals I had to endure. He is worth every drop of tears I shed over him and each sleepless night I spent with him on my mind.

From that moment on, my life takes a new direction. Not completely new, actually. Ace and I continue loving each other fiercely and fill our days with getting to know each other... and with lots of sex.

Epilogue

I move in with Ace and we have a road trip across the country, finishing our travel in Las Vegas, barely making it to Chloe's wedding with Dylan. The day after the wedding, I wake up with a phone call from Adam, informing me about Taylor's two-weeks-too-early labor the previous night. Now I'm a proud aunt of twin girls.

Ace proposes to me on our first year anniversary, and we marry in a small wedding with family and friends and travel to Europe for our honeymoon, starting from Barcelona, ending in Prague. When I give him my wedding present, he embraces me tightly in a bear hug and whispers into my ear that I'm the one for him, tears accompanying his words.

'What wedding surprise?' you will ask. You'll be surprised to hear it's actually another woman, namely, his birth mother.

At the end of our honeymoon, I convince him to detour to a new destination, St Petersburg, and contact his mother, the renowned physics professor, Alexa Averin. She meets us for a tear-filled dinner, where patrons at the nearby tables eye us curiously while we, three adults, cry our eyes out.

Ace recites to her everything he can manage about his life in a three-hour meeting, leaving out most of the tidbits related to the physical and emotional abuses he had to endure while growing up with his adoptive family.

Alexa resigns from her job at the San Petersburg State University the next month to take a faculty position in the physics department at UCLA and buys the apartment right next door to us to make up for the time she lost with her son.

After over two decades of solitude, she has so much love to give. She instantly takes over her role as a mother, not only to Ace, but to me as well, feeding us both with immense love and affection and being there for us as our rock during the last decades of her life.

Even Taylor and Adam start seeing her as a mother figure and consult with her about everything and anything regarding their children, business, house, holiday plans, and what not, and Alexa ever so patiently and lovingly guides them toward the right direction.

The bombshell comes the day after the Californian gubernatorial election and Edward Neuberger is elected to be the next governor. Zane tactfully tips the police about a video tape he recorded years ago of Edward while he was sexually abusing Ace, causing one of the biggest media scandals related to a politician, perhaps only second after the Bill Clinton-Monica Lewinsky incident.

The footages of Edward while he's taken out, handcuffed and horrified, from the celebration party of his election victory and later his trial occupy the news for several weeks. He receives a twenty-year sentence and dies after an attack by a religious fanatic in the prison.

Zane, being Zane, tags along, dozens of women with him, before finally tying the knot with no other than Julie, his accomplice in Michael's ruin. Knowing every little detail about Zane's campaign of destruction, Julie uses her influence to gain an executive role in HMG and soon becomes Zane's advisor.

Zane pursues her obsessively for months for a date.

After that first date, the rest is history. She turns him into a love-blind puppy and ends up having a whopping five children with him. But not without making him go through a series of humbling tests and trials to prove his worthiness and having him beg for each and every step into their union that culminates in marriage.

How do I know about the humiliating tests? Julie and I have become very good friends.

With Chloe, not so much.

She still creeps me out with her unusual remarks and weird attitude, and I think she holds a secret grudge against me for stealing her little brother from her.

As for my career, I leave HMG after completing the full year and with a part of the one point eight million dollars I've earned, I set up my own data-analysis consulting firm and, the very next day after its founding, get contracted by HMG's marketing department.

I also pursue a PhD degree in statistics and attend the graduation ceremony with my belly nearly reaching up my nose.

Our baby girl decides to show us her beautiful face on July the 7th, the day of my mother's death and my birthday. Now I have no choice but lose my fear of seven and keep my eyes open for the wonders that are associated with it. Ace and I go on having two more girls and move to a big house with a backyard the size of a football field in the same neighborhood with Taylor.

Pleasure Extraordinaire continues to be a successful business venture, but Ace decides to sell it on his thirtieth birthday and embarks on a career in real estate with again very profitable outcomes.

Our once heated and unstable relationship grows into one of continued happiness with mutual trust and unending love, and we hang on to each other until the end no matter what life throws at us.

Epilogue - ACE

Lindsay, the only balm to my scarred soul.

She made me a man. She made me a father. She taught me how to love and trust. Helped me find myself and become the content and confident me I am today. And she had the grace to attribute the improvements in me to the therapy.

That was the only lie I ever told her in our fifty years of togetherness. I stopped going to therapy after the first appointment, because I didn't see a need for it. Not when I had the cure right by my side, sharing my bed, wrapping her arms possessively around my neck, giving me sloppy, wet kisses, whispering her love to me, over and over again, looking at me like I'm the king of the world, God's ultimate gift to her.

I may have had shit happen to me during the first part of my life, but I wouldn't want to change a thing because whatever pain I suffered also brought her to me.

And since she became my girlfriend, then my wife, and the mother of my children, my life rocked each and every day. I'm grateful for the day that fierce girl sat on the chair in front of me in my office in Pleasure Extraordinaire and giggled her way through my obscene interview questions.

I'm grateful that I'm one of those few lucky people who got to find his soul mate and keep her for a very long time, waking up next to her and seeing the world through her eyes, sharing with her the sorrows and the true miracles of life.

Our three babies all turned into intelligent, committed, strong, and caring adults. Any other way would be impossible with the mother they have. And we tasted the overwhelming joy of becoming grandparents.

Now, well into our seventies, Lindsay and I are kicking it every day and looking forward to another decade or two of love and support. Early morning biking and lazy afternoons. Wines and hugs. Gardening and pillow fights. Laughter and peace. And an infinite number of kisses.

With Lindsay, I'm living life the way it should be. Truly happy.

THE END

Pleasure Extraordinaire - ZANE

By Liv Bennett

Chapter 1 - On The Road

"I can't be with you, Zane. I'm in love with your brother."

Her hair black and wild, her lips red and swollen, she wipes the tears away. Not hers, but mine. My fucking tears for the wasted opportunity to be with the one and only woman who could make me want to give up everything.

How could I have been so stupid not to realize she was the one, before my bastard brother and nemesis, Ace, snatched her from me?

I saw her first. I flirted with her first and she returned my advances. I fucked her first. But I didn't treat her like she deserved right from the beginning. That's where I lost the game. And that's why the nightmares about her declaring her love for my bastard brother wake me up in a sweat more often than I can handle.

I need a scotch. A bottle of scotch to numb my brain. 158 goddamn days have passed since the day I realized she's gone for good. 158 days of torturous life that I've had to endure.

I scan the interior of the car I've been dozing off in and realize the car isn't moving. Pushing the button to lower the separator between me and my chauffeur, Dane, I ask him what the problem is.

"There seems to be a car accident at the Santa Monica and Wilshire crossing, sir," he replies, looking apologetic as if he caused the accident.

I exhale a long breath of frustration and glance down at my watch. Half an hour before my first appointment of the week. I'd better call Julie to reschedule it since the traffic doesn't seem to be moving anytime soon. A jolt of headache runs from my head down to my neck, making me wince with pain. The longer I sit here doing nothing, the more painful the headache will get. Restless and angry, I climb out of the car and text Julie to inform her about my tardiness.

As soon as I step on the sidewalk, two young blonde girls giggle loudly and rush toward me. "Zane Hawkins!" they cheer in chorus, making a few heads turn with their high-pitched voices.

"Hi." I smile and glance down at my phone. I may not be a rock star or an A-list actor but I get as much, or maybe even more attention from ladies as any big-name celebrity.

I'm the fucking owner and the CEO of Hawkins Media Group that earned half a billion dollars in annual revenues just last year. I'm also the creator, producer, and occasional director of the top-rated and highly popular TV show, Frat House. My resume alone would get me laid on a daily basis if I were a ninety-year old dude with a breathing tube hanging down my face, saggy tits and wrinkly penis, but let's just say that's not the case.

The two girls stand before me, too close for strangers to be, but I've never minded female attention and today is no different. Both have long blonde hair down to their elbows, one curly and the other one straight as corn husk.

The curly haired one is wearing a short, pink summer dress which displays her long legs rather deliciously. The other girl has obviously skipped wearing a bra and her nipples form nice buds beneath her low-cut blouse.

"I'm Beverly," the curly haired girl says eagerly. "And this is Teresa. We're big fans of Frat House. We know every line, every scene."

"Well, lucky you. I happen to have tickets for the shooting of the next episode." Putting my phone into the pocket of my dress pants, I grab my wallet from my other pocket and slip out the tickets.

Their eyes widen and they start jumping up and down on the street, clapping their hands and screaming, "Oh, my God!" over and over again.

I smile as I hand them their tickets. "Don't forget to follow our Twitter and Facebook pages."

"We're already on both." Beverly snatches the tickets from my hand and throws herself at me, I assume, to show her gratitude.

I neither hug her back nor pull myself away from her enthusiastic embrace, just focusing on the press of her ample boobs against my chest, as I let my eyes wonder over Teresa's breasts. Her nipples harden visibly, and as I move my gaze over her face and smile, I realize she's blushing, obviously aware of my intense study of her beautiful body.

They both look so young, I doubt they're legally adults. Their pussies must be used very little and tight as a glove. As much as I'd love sink into their eager cunts, I'd rather not spend the rest of my life in prison as a sex offender for screwing underage kids.

I move away out of Beverly's hold slowly and nod my head at them. "I guess it's time for me to go." I glance down at my car and realize it hasn't moved an inch.

"No, don't go yet," Beverly calls out and grabs my hand. "The traffic will take a while."

"Yeah, it will. Why don't you get us a room at the Beverly Hilton and chill with us rather than wasting your time in your car?" Teresa asks and motions with her chin toward the Beverly Hilton hotel a few feet away down the road.

"Yeah, we'll make it worth your time. I promise," Beverly adds eagerly.

"Well, I'm not sure." I scratch the back of my head, studying the luscious bodies of both girls.

They're both fair-skinned and slim, except for their perky breasts and relatively toned hips. Teresa's stomach is flat beneath her blouse and makes me want to lick all over her smooth skin until I dip my tongue into her pussy.

My cock stirs with the thoughts of enjoying two innocent-looking girls. A sweaty fucking session is definitely a better way to start the day than a glass of scotch, but there's still the problem with their ages. "How old are you?"

"Oh, don't worry about that. We're both nineteen." Teresa quickly produces her driver's license and hands it to me. Beverly follows suit. Their ages check out, which means there's no obstacle between my cock and their pussies.

"All right, then. You, go ahead and wait for me in the lobby. I'll be a minute."

They nod their heads in response and start running down the street, which gives me a chance to check out their asses. Both nice and firm. This is going to be fun.

After ordering Dane to drive to the parking lot of the hotel, I head for the reception desk and hand my credit card to the middle-aged, brunette receptionist. She smiles at me in recognition and quickly reserves a suite for me, and all the while I wonder if I should add her into my little morning play.

She makes sure our hands touch as she gives me my card back, and I wink at her along with a playful smile, but dismiss the idea of having her in order to spare myself the trouble of having to explain to her about Teresa and Beverly.

"Have a great day," the receptionist wishes me as I turn toward the elevators and find my girls giggling.

"He's so hot." I hear Teresa whispering and Beverly nods her head several times, her chest moving up and down way too quickly.

I place my hands at the small of their backs and guide them toward the elevator under the curious eyes of the other hotel guests. As soon as the elevator doors close on us, Teresa wraps her arms around me and pushes her lips against mine. While exploring her mouth, I feel Beverly rubbing her body against the side of my body, her hands immediately landing on my growing erection.

These girls are nothing but innocent and I have no complaints whatsoever about it.

We practically run to my suite, and while I run the key to open the door, Teresa already starts unbuttoning her blouse, her eyes locked on my face, her bottom lip between her teeth. My phone buzzes as I open the door. The girls walk into the bedroom and I glance down at the screen of my phone to see Julie's calling.

Declining the call and turning off the phone, I slide out of my jacket and watch as the girls slowly undress before me. Teresa's blouse lands on the floor first. Her breasts are big and firm, better than I'd imagined, her nipples are hard and require my immediate attention.

Beverly quickly makes up for lost time and pulls her

dress over her head, standing with a light-pink bra and a tiny triangle of thong before me.

I go for Teresa nonetheless and unbutton and unzip her jeans and quickly slip my hand beneath her panties to feel her soaking pussy. She moans while I slide my finger between her pussy lips.

Beverly mirrors my behavior and works on the zipper of my pants, pushing them down along with my boxer briefs. My cock springs free in full size, ready to fuck the brains out of these two girls.

While Teresa rides my hand to her first orgasm in loud moans, Beverly kneels in front of me and parts her plum red lips, looking impatient to prove her oral skills.

Teresa's pussy vibrates around my fingers, and Beverly quickly mouths my cock to its base, gagging as my cock hits the depths of her throat.

Teresa might have the bigger breasts and better body, but it's Beverly that now has my full focus thanks to her eager sucking. I drop Teresa and run my hands through Beverly's thick curls to hold her in place while I pump hard into her mouth. She's unquestionably an expert at cock-sucking and reminds me of the only other excellent cock sucker I know of—Lindsay.

Fuck! I shouldn't go there. Not now. Not ever.

Angry at myself for letting thoughts of Lindsay get into my head, I push Beverly's head back and release myself from her mouth. She falls on her butt and looks up at me in shock and hesitation.

"Get on your feet and bend down in front of the bed. Both of you," I order.

Both girls get out of the last pieces of clothing and walk fully naked toward the bed and as ordered, line up at the end of it and bend down, displaying their firm asses and swollen, pink pussies to me. Their breasts hang down, their skin and hair glowing under the dim light flowing through the curtains.

Grabbing two condoms out of my wallet, I sheath my cock with one and position myself behind Teresa. My eyes trail the crevice between her ass cheeks down the pulsating folds of her pussy and her glistering juices. I land my hands on each cheek and spread them apart, watching the muscles around her back opening clench in response.

"Have you ever been fucked in the ass?" I ask.

"No," Teresa replies.

"I have." Beverly interferes with my interaction with Teresa, looking at me over her shoulder. "I love anal."

I give her an appreciative smile and push the head of my cock into Teresa's pussy. She's as tight as I imagined and the evidence of her arousal lubes my condom-clad cock generously. Her hands fall on the edge of the bed as I pump into her, harder with each second. Even Beverly's jealous glare can't stop her from moaning in pleasure and soon her pussy starts pulsating with wild quivers.

Smiling at myself with satisfaction, I push myself out of Teresa and slip the used condom off and roll on a new one for Beverly. She lets out a squeak of excitement and pulls her legs together, pushing her hips higher in the air, ready to catch my cock.

"I don't carry lube with me," I say.

"That's okay. I'm wet enough in my pussy," Beverly explains between her ragged breaths.

I run a finger between the lips of her pussy to check her explanation although her glistering juices can be detected from a mile away.

Pushing the lips of her sex aside with my fingers, I ease into her opening and listen to her exaggerated moans as I inch deeper inside her. She's tighter than Teresa, which makes me curious as to how much tighter she'll be in the ass. After two strokes, I slip out and push the head of my cock against her ass opening, glancing at Teresa briefly while she's now lying on her back on the bed, her hands playing with her breasts. She's clearly aware of the beauty of those firm globes and uses it to her advantage to steal my attention from her friend.

Girls and the competition between them…makes for an incredible sexual adventure.

As much as I enjoy watching Teresa, I my eyes land back on Beverly's ass so I won't hurt her butt in the process. True to her words, Beverly opens up for me, and I ease into her with only a slight protest of her tight muscles. I'm a goner for anal, and her eagerness to have me inside her ass, puts her ahead of the game.

That and her loud moans. I'd consider taking her as my lover if I hadn't been already dealing with a couple of dozen.

The tightness of her ass around my shaft makes it hard for me to prolong my erection, but I owe her at least an orgasm for offering her ass to me, not to mention that Teresa got two. Moving my hand down, I press my fingers against Beverly's clit and rub it first gently then intensify the pressure. In a matter seconds, she climaxes in my hand, her even louder moans echoing against the four walls of the large suite.

I hear Teresa chuckling while my eyes close, my own climax only a few pumps away. Holding Beverly's hips with both hands, I thrust harder into her and explode inside the condom, feeling my heart beating against my ears.

As soon as the last drip of sperm is out, my attraction to the two girls hits bottom, and a feeling of disgust surfaces. I slip out of Beverly and walk toward the trash can while getting the shit-covered condom off and throw it into the can.

I consider hopping into the bathtub for a quick shower but the girls look too eager to leave it only with one round, and I'd rather not fuck someone whose name I'll forget in an hour, for a second time, so I only wash my hands and hurry to put on my clothes.

"Enjoy the suite for the day and order whatever you want. It's on me," I say as I walk toward the door without even looking back to see what they're up to. I hear them saying good bye and close the door.

Twenty minutes of fun with two pretty girls without any strings attached. That's exactly how a satisfying sexual encounter should be, minus the feeling of disgust that's ruining my good mood. I didn't have it before Lindsay. Gone are the days I used to just feel good and carry on with my daily life after a good round of sex.

I guess it's the curse of falling in love with the wrong woman… or falling in love altogether.

Chapter 2 - On The Market

Julie stands as I enter her office. She's not just my secretary but also my long-time accomplice in my successful effort to rid myself of my father and take over the reins of Hawkins Media Group. Clad in a long, black skirt-suit, she holds her black cup of coffee in her hand, her eyebrows tightly pulled together into an angry furrow.

I don't remember the last time she had a different color on. Perhaps before my mother's death more than a decade ago? But at that time, I didn't care enough about her to even notice what she was wearing. Over the years she's become such a big part of my professional and private life, she's practically irreplaceable. Hawkins Media Group could survive without me running it, but without Julie, it wouldn't even make it a full year.

"I'd really appreciate it if you didn't decline my calls," she says in her usual feverish way. "James had an urgent matter to discuss with you about the next episode's scenario. Apparently one of the writers went into labor last night and we need to find a replacement for her very quickly." She doesn't sound pleased at my rudeness for declining her calls, obviously, but there's something else, something out of the ordinary beneath her anger.

My eyes travel over her face up to the tight bun on the top of her head, I slip my hands into the pockets of my pants and look down at her. "What about the other writers on the team? Ask them to work overtime to compensate for the lost hours. They won't be the first team to work a few extra hours in the entertainment industry." The only reason I'm yelling at her, rather than speaking softly is because she's one of the few women I know of, who won't collapse on their desk in tears, but rather push my button for a heated discussion.

And, as expected, she narrows her eyes at me in an angrier fashion, sizing me up and down for my power, although clearly I'm her boss and my power is omniscient. "You're probably not aware of the tiny little fact that they're already working a hundred hours a week and not getting paid for their extra work."

"Well, then pay them for the extra hours so they'll shut up and do their work properly."

"Sir, with all due respect, I seriously think we need to hire one or two more writers. With their workload, the current writers will burn out very soon and we'll lose the momentum of the series. I have already identified three candidates and can schedule an interview with them for the afternoon." She grabs a file from her desk and extends it to me.

Smiling, I shake my head, ignoring the file she's holding before my face. "Since when do you call me sir?"

Her cheeks blush, perhaps for the first time in the sixteen years that I've known her, making my grin grow wider. "Zane," she corrects her mistake and adds, "You should really take a look at the profiles of the candidates and interview them as soon as possible."

"Nah. I'll pass. You interview them."

Her eyebrows raise in excitement; her lips part in surprise. "Really?"

"Come on! You've been my right arm through thick

and thin against my father. You can manage a boring interview now, can't you?"

"Of course, I can. I just didn't think you'd trust me with those issues."

I smirk and walk toward my office door. "You clearly don't know how much I trust you. I could practically leave the entire corporation to you and I have no doubt you'd run it as well as I do." Perhaps even better, but she doesn't need to know that.

Looking over my shoulder as I open the door to my office, I see her smile in confidence. "Can you get me a cup of coffee?"

Her good mood sours visibly as she looks at me with a disappointed expression.

I laugh. "Just kidding. I'll drink scotch. Want to join me?"

"Zane, please don't do that. With the amount of alcohol you're consuming, you're going to end up becoming an alcoholic. Don't do it to yourself." She plops into her chair when I don't respond to her worry-filled warning and just walk into my office.

Of course she's right, but I have yet to figure out any other way to get over the pain. So I drink to make it go away…even if it works only for a moment.

Confused about how I'll pass the morning without liqueur clouding my mind, I settle on my chair and notice the pile of magazines I'm sure Julie set out for me. Picking up one, I study the cover with my picture with Penelope on it.

"Zane Hawkins, the CEO and the owner of Hawkins Media Group, is officially dating to marry," says the title of the LA Celebrity News magazine.

Rolling my eyes at the utter craziness of the possibility of me marrying, I flip through the pages and find the article to read it to see what bullshit the creative journalist came up with about me this time.

After two years of on-again-off-again romance with the actress Penelope Davis, Zane Hawkins is now ready to settle down. Multiple sources confirm that it's the recent death of his father, Michael Hawkins, that made him re-think his bachelor lifestyle and consider starting a family of his own.

I chuckle, despite the irritation I get every time I'm reminded of my father, and call out for Julie.

"Have you read this bullshit?" I ask, although I have no doubt she has not only read and memorized each line written about me in the media, but also carefully reviewed the piece for its appropriateness before its publication. She's a perfectionist when it comes to her job, but one of her best qualities is she never leaves a misbehaving journalist or blogger unpunished. I'd say she gets an extra satisfaction for getting the company attorney to send out cease-and-desist orders if I didn't know her real satisfaction comes from bothering me.

Still holding her cup of coffee, she steps into my office and slides elegantly into the chair before my desk, her face brightly lit with a sly smile "Bullshit? You're breaking my heart. What's bullshit about it?"

"Everything. None of it is true."

"Oh. Would you have rather it say 'after his recent failure to win the heart of the girl he loved and consequently losing her to his brother, Zane is fucking everything with a hole to mend his broken heart?'"

I chuckle to keep my cool and also to show her I'm not affected by her words that are nothing but the truth. "I should have never told you anything about Lindsay." Even voicing her name tightens my chest in pain, and the thought of the loving looks she gives to Ace floods through my mind.

Julie's smile gives way to a warm, yet sad, expression. "You didn't need to tell me—I knew it before you even realized you were falling for her."

"Really?" Can't a man have a few secrets to himself?

She nods and sips from her coffee.

I pick another random magazine among the pile of nonsense and read the title on the cover. "Five things Zane Hawkins is looking for in a wife." I read it out loud and lift my gaze to her, trying my best not to laugh at the ridiculousness of the title. "Do you know the five things I'm looking for in a wife, too?"

She covers her mouth with a hand while chuckling. "That was just to increase the ratings of Frat House, and I admit, it was a lot of fun coming up with the bullet points."

I scan the article before me, shaking my head at the complete absurdity of each point that supposedly represents my requirements for a woman who would carry my name. "She should be able to cook and bake. Really? That's the number one requirement? Not fantastic oral skills or possession of a great booty?"

She rolls her eyes at me disapprovingly. "Great skills or some fat ass won't feed your children. And please don't tell me you have the iron chef cooking your meals for you. Nothing beats food cooked with love. Would you want your future kids to eat food cooked by their mom or by some restaurant chef?"

Without commenting on her valid argument, I proceed to the second point on the article. "She should believe in God. That can't be real. I don't even remember the last time I went to church."

"During your mother's funeral," she reminds me and adds. "I didn't come up with this one, I promise. It was your mom's idea."

"My mom's? My dead mom's idea?"

"Yeah, well. She made me promise her a variety of things before…you know…she took her own life. And one of the promises was that I'd help you find a truly God-fearing woman for a wife."

"What else did she make you promise?"

She bites her lower lip. "I'd rather not say."

Any conversation regarding my mother and her death by suicide is off topic, which is why I continue with the article rather than pushing Julie to spill her secrets. "Unselfish, undemanding and independent. Finally something I'd value in a woman."

"I'm glad I could get you to agree on at least one point."

"She should be hundred percent loyal to me. This one is absolutely true, but it should be actually the number one requirement. She should be loyal to me as a man and as a partner in life."

Julie's lips curl up and part in a wide smile, contentment and pride clear in her face. "Gosh, I so knew you'd say that." She stands, walking around my desk, and stops next to me, glancing down at the magazine in my hands.

I freeze for a moment as the scent of her perfume hits me. Honey suckle.

Her perfume is the only feminine quality she has, and each time I get to smell it, my body stills momentarily and I'm reminded of the fact that she's not just some employee or a good friend, but also a woman with breasts and vagina beneath her unflattering clothes.

"Why don't you for once wear something sexy?" I ask, completely forgetting about the context of my relationship with her.

Her face turns sad in an instant and her eyes fall on the desk. "You wouldn't ask me that question if you knew about the things your father forced me to do."

My whole body tenses, and I wince at her words and form fists with my hands, wanting to hit myself for reminding her of the evil ways of my father. I'm well aware of the things she had to go through as my father's assistant for several years, but I have no idea why she's stayed for so long. Was that also a part of her promise to my mother?

"I'm very sorry." I turn my head down to the magazine to change the topic and hopefully to make her forget about the painful past. "Be sexually open-minded," I read the last item and laugh. "That's my girl!" I shout with an extra note of cheerfulness to distract her. "You indeed know me well."

"You work as a gigolo at Pleasure Extraordinaire. I figured you'd be a total waste of time for a virgin or a prude."

Ah yes, my part-time work at the brothel that caters to women. The place that widens my horizons about women. Not just fashion models or movie actresses, but I get to enjoy a large variety of women, anything from bored housewives and CEOs, to cougars, Latinas...you name it. The world of Pleasure Extraordinaire is filled with delightful surprises.

Julie draws in a long breath of air and lands her eyes on me, still looking bothered. "Now you know you're officially looking for a wife to marry. I'll set up a list of appropriate women for you to date, but feel free to let me know if you have someone special in mind that you want to get to know." She pauses and locks her eyes on mine, looking as if she's expecting me to come up with a name this instant.

"Ahhh," I mumble, still trying to soak in the idea of marriage. "I don't think it's a good idea. Realistically speaking, I won't marry, and even if I do by some miracle, I'm not born to be a monogamous man. I love women as in plural."

"No man is born to be monogamous. It's what you choose to become for the woman you love and the family you will form. Look, you're pushing thirty-three. The quality of your sperm is diminishing each passing day and you're wasting your good sperm on flings and one-night stands, rather than making babies and continuing your legacy."

"Excuse me! My sperm is in perfect shape," I correct her, rather insulted by her insinuation. No one has the right to offend my manhood, not even Julie.

She exhales loudly as if trying to keep herself from arguing with my statement. "I promised your mother I'd take care of Chloe, Ace, and you. Both Chloe and Ace have found their partners and neither need my help anymore. You're the only burden on my shoulders. You have to find a wife and start a family so I can complete my mission and start my own life. I'm tired of babysitting you."

"I don't need you taking care of me. I'm a grown man in case you haven't noticed."

"I don't care." She takes a step closer to me, her eyebrows pulled together, her eyes narrowed. "Irene was one of the very few people who impacted my life and I won't turn my back on her by breaking my promise. You'll find an appropriate woman and marry her by the end of the year, even better if you can knock her up within the first few months of your marriage..." She lifts her hand and points her index finger toward me "...or so help me I'll ruin your reputation so badly no woman will ever want to so much as touch you."

"Spare your energy. Nothing you can say or do will convince me." I push my chair back with my feet to keep a safe distance between her and me.

"Oh, yeah? How about this? Thirty years from now. You will be sixty-two and won't be in the best shape to run a billion-dollar company. Who do you think will take over control? Who will be the next owner and CEO of Hawkins Media Group? Let me answer it for you. One of Ace's children. Is that what you what? You lost the woman you loved to Ace. Do you really want to lose the legacy of HMG to his offspring as well? Think about it for a moment."

She might be right. I never wanted him to be part of my family, and I'll do everything to keep his children away from taking over the company my own father founded. I might hate Michael for a variety of reasons, but I won't deny his hard work and the sacrifices he made to make the company what it is today.

I let out a long breath of defeat and shrug my acceptance. Julie is right. I need a beautiful, sexy and honorable woman to bear and raise my children and I need her now!

Julie's angry face turns into a scary kind of happy in a heartbeat. "Good! I'll email you the list."

About the Author

Liv Bennett lives in California with her husband, daughter, and two loud budgies. Reading and writing erotic romance are her favorite forms of relaxation, in addition to long walks and yoga. She's a social drinker of coffee, but a serious tea addict.

Sign up to get alerts about her upcoming releases
eepurl.com/F_nqD
https://www.facebook.com/LivBennettAuthor
(Please log into Facebook before clicking on this link)
slivbennett@gmail.com

Made in the USA
Coppell, TX
22 June 2022

79133068R00104